Murder in Cairo

A LOTTIE SPRIGG MYSTERY BOOK 3

MARTHA BOND

The Lottie Sprigg Mystery Series

~

Murder in Venice
Murder in Paris
Murder in Cairo
Murder in Monaco

Murder in Cairo

Chapter One

LORD HARBOTTLE HELD onto his hat as the motorcycle sped along the dusty street. Then he jolted forward as it braked to a sudden halt.

'Good grief, Villiers, are you trying to catapult me out of this thing?'

'No such luck this time,' replied Benjamin Villiers as he climbed off the motorcycle and opened the door of the sidecar so Lord Harbottle could clamber out.

'So this is the place, is it?' Lord Harbottle made his way to the steps of the Kursaal Music Hall, a simple two-storey building of cream stone. The place seemed unfamiliar to him in the bright sunshine. 'Are you sure this is where we were last night?'

'Absolutely sure.'

'It looks different.'

'Probably because we're sober.'

'Speak for yourself, Villiers, I didn't drink that much.'

The windows were shuttered against the heat of the after-noon, and the entrance door was locked when Lord Harbottle tried the handle. 'I don't think there's anyone inside,' he said.

'She must be here, she's not at the hotel.'

Lord Harbottle rapped his knuckles against the door. 'Miss Omar!' Silence followed and he mopped his brow with his handkerchief while he waited for a reply. 'Warm isn't it, Villiers? What do you suppose it is today? Ninety?'

'I'd say so.'

Hot and impatient, Lord Harbottle knocked on the door again. 'Miss Omar! Are you in there? It's Lord Harbottle!' He hoped the mention of his name might provoke some urgency.

'You could telephone her,' said Villiers.

'No, this is a conversation which must be face-to-face. She's ignoring me, isn't she? It won't do. I shall have to return this evening and create a scene if she refuses to open this door.'

'I wouldn't do that, Harbottle.'

'But something has to be done! I can't just — oh, good afternoon, Miss Omar!'

Lord Harbottle doffed his hat at the lady who'd just opened the door. She was dark-skinned with pencil-thin eyebrows and beautiful dark eyes. She wore a long embroidered robe and her hair was covered in a tangerine scarf. Large beaded earrings jangled at her jawline.

'May I have a word?' he asked.

IT TOOK a while for Lord Harbottle's eyes to adjust from the brightness of the street to the dim interior of the club, and he knocked his shin on a chair as he followed Mayar Omar across the nightclub floor. A musty odour of stale tobacco smoke lingered in the air. The stage, which had hosted an array of dancers and performers the previous night, now looked small and shabby.

'I'll wait here,' said Villiers. He sat at a table and lit a cigarette.

Miss Omar's office was furnished in polished mahogany with colourful carpets on the walls and floor.

'How can I help, Lord Harbottle?' She took a seat behind her desk and gave him a smile so enchanting that he was almost distracted from his thoughts.

'I'd like to say that I enjoyed myself enormously here yesterday evening.'

'Good.' She smiled again. 'We aim to please.'

'You certainly do that alright.'

Miss Omar impressed him. Not only was she beautiful, but she was clever and a talented performer, too. She spoke five languages: English, French, Arabic, Persian and Turkish. She'd been born in Syria and worked as an actress and dancer in Beirut before moving to Cairo and embarking on her career as a nightclub owner.

'Is there anything else?' she asked.

'Yes, er... yes, actually there is.' He smoothed his moustache. 'There was a photographer in the club yesterday evening.'

'That's right.'

'I believe he may have taken some photographs of me. In fact, I know he did because he practically blinded me with that flash lamp of his. He should warn people before firing that thing off, you know. Why was he taking photographs?'

'We like to take photographs of our guests enjoying themselves. We use some of the best pictures in our promotional literature.'

Lord Harbottle felt a pang of alarm. 'You won't be using any photographs of *me* in your promotions, will you?'

'Would you not like that?'

'Absolutely not! No.' Unfortunately for Lord Harbottle, an attractive dancer had been sitting on his knee when the photographs had been taken. 'Is there any way of obtaining the photographs? I can pay good money for them if need be.'

'We don't sell our photographs, Lord Harbottle, we merely use them for our own purposes.'

'Ah, but I would be in terrible trouble, you see, if those photographs fell into the wrong hands.'

'They won't fall into the wrong hands.'

'How can you be sure of that?' As much as he admired Miss Omar, he wasn't sure he could trust her.

'I pride myself on being discreet.' She gave another dazzling smile. 'As do all my staff. If you're worried your wife might see the photographs, then I can assure you she won't.'

He gave a splutter at the unexpected mention of his wife. 'Good! Because even though I've done absolutely nothing wrong, it may not look that way in the photographs.'

'Of course.'

'The fact of the matter is, my wife doesn't even know I attended this nightclub last night. She thought I was at the Turf Club. And indeed, I was at the Turf Club until Villiers dragged me here. It was all his idea.'

'But you enjoyed yourself, didn't you, Lord Harbottle?'

'Yes, I did.' He sighed. 'Is there really no possible way I can obtain those photographs? I'm a peer of the realm, I have a lot of influence. If there's anything you need at all, I can arrange it.' What else could he say to persuade her? Most people would have agreed to his request by now.

'I shall have a conversation with the photographer.'

'And?'

'I shall see what he says.'

This wasn't the answer he'd been hoping for. 'It's imperative that you do, Miss Omar. Because if any of those photographs ever fall into the wrong hands, then I shall...'

'What, Lord Harbottle?'

'I can't hold myself responsible for what might happen.'

'I REALISE it's unladylike to admit it,' said Mrs Moore. 'But my clothes are sticking to me.' She pulled at her high-collared blouse, then wafted her fan over her face. 'I do hope I get accustomed to this heat soon. Who'd have thought Cairo could be so hot in April?'

Lottie agreed. She was tempted to suggest to her employer that she'd be cooler if she abandoned her Edwardian blouses and skirts and wore something light and modern instead.

They sat on the terrace of Shepheard's Hotel, an elegant stone building which wouldn't have looked out of place in Paris or London. The terrace was laid out with tables and wicker chairs and overlooked a tree-lined street. A tall wooden portico provided some shade from the sun, as did the spreading leaves of large potted palms.

Waiters in white robes and red fez hats busied around the tables. The guests were mainly well-dressed Europeans and Americans, but there were wealthy Arab guests too and a few men in various military uniforms. Although they'd only recently arrived in Cairo, Lottie had noticed the city hosted people from all over the world.

Lottie sipped her glass of cool lemonade and her Pembroke Welsh Corgi, Rosie, lay in the shade beneath the table, panting gently. She was growing accustomed to the heat but wasn't as lively as usual.

'You're a new one!' said a grey-haired lady at a neighbouring table.

'Who? Me?' said Mrs Moore.

'Yes, you.' The lady's lined face made Lottie think of a lizard or a tortoise. She wore an old-fashioned black dress embellished with buttons and lace and sparkling rings adorned her long, bony fingers. 'Have you just arrived?'

'Yes I have,' replied Mrs Moore. 'This morning, in fact. I'm Mrs Roberta Moore.'

'You're American.'

'Yes, the daughter of a railroad tycoon.'

'A tycoon?' The old lady raised an eyebrow.

'Yes, I grew up in Pennsylvania. My sister is married to Lord Buckley-Phipps and they live in Shropshire in England. Fortescue Manor. Have you heard of it?'

'No.'

'I only asked because you sound English.'

'I am.'

'There seem to be a lot of English people in this hotel.'

'Well that's only natural, isn't it?'

'Is it?'

'Yes, Egypt was under British control for forty years and this hotel could almost be in Mayfair or Piccadilly, couldn't it? Except for the glorious weather that is. Is this your daughter?' She pointed a bony finger at Lottie.

'No, she's my assistant Lottie Sprigg. She used to work as a maid for my sister.'

'Hello Lottie.'

'And our dog Rosie is dozing underneath the table.'

The old lady craned her head to have a look. 'So she is.

How lovely. I'm Mrs Margaret de Vere. Delighted to make your acquaintance. Have you been to Cairo before?'

'No, it's lovely to come somewhere new. I've travelled here to meet an acquaintance of mine, Prince Manfred of Bavaria.'

The prince was considered to be the most eligible bachelor in Europe and Mrs Moore intended to make him her fourth husband. Having encountered him briefly in Venice and Paris, she was hoping she would see more of him in Cairo.

'Oh, you know the prince?' said Mrs de Vere. 'Poor chap. Hopefully he'll recover soon.'

'Recover?'

'Haven't you heard? He's terribly unwell.'

'*Terribly*? I didn't know! Is it serious?'

'I don't know.'

'It's not malaria, is it?'

'I couldn't tell you, I'm afraid. There's a doctor here at the hotel looking after him, and I think a nurse has been found as well. I'm sure it's nothing to worry about, in fact, it's not uncommon to fall unwell when acclimatising to the tropics. This climate doesn't suit everyone, you know.'

'How long are you staying here?'

'I live here. I've been here for two years.'

'Golly, that long?'

'Cairo is my home now, I'm quite settled here and have a maid who looks after me. I'm here on doctor's orders. The damp English weather was playing havoc with my joints, so the doctor prescribed me sunshine.'

'What a wonderful thing to be prescribed.'

'I can't complain. Are you married, Mrs Moore?'

'No, I'm divorced. My last husband ran off with a dancer.'

'Oh dear.'

'It was for the best. I don't have a great deal of luck with husbands. My first died of rheumatic fever and my second died of drink.'

'That's very unlucky indeed. I feel so fortunate that my late husband was the love of my life. Oh look who it is! Lord Harbottle and Mr Villiers.'

Two men were ascending the steps to the terrace, both wearing smart linen suits. The older of the two was tall and lean and had a neat grey moustache. He carried a horsehair fly whisk in one hand. The younger man looked about thirty and had a suntanned complexion.

Mrs de Vere's table was located in the perfect spot for her to grab the men's attention as they approached.

'Come and join us!' she called out to them.

'I'm just about to freshen up,' said the older man.

'That can wait,' said Mrs de Vere. 'Come and meet a new guest, Mrs Moore, she's the daughter of an American tycoon. We can pull these tables together.' She instructed a waiter to do so and, a moment later, all five of them were sitting together.

'Lord and Lady Harbottle have just been on a trip to Luxor with Mr Villiers,' explained Mrs de Vere. 'He's an archaeologist.'

'Are you indeed?' said Mrs Moore. 'You must be extremely knowledgeable.'

His grin revealed two rows of neat white teeth. 'I do my best.'

'You gentlemen look rather hot and bothered,' said Mrs de Vere. 'It's foolish to be gallivanting about during the warmest part of the day.'

'Business called,' said Lord Harbottle, flicking at the air with his fly whisk.

'What sort of business?'

'If I tell you, then every single guest in Shepheard's will know by the end of the day.' Lord Harbottle leaned in to Mrs Moore. 'Mrs de Vere is an irrepressible gossip.'

'Nonsense!' said Mrs de Vere.

'Don't tell her a thing,' he added. 'You'll regret it.'

'I consider it most ungentlemanly to talk about a lady in that manner,' said Mrs de Vere. 'You should be ashamed of yourself, Lord Harbottle.'

Lottie felt uncomfortable, unsure if she was speaking seriously or in jest.

'Ah, now here's my darling wife!' said Lord Harbottle as an attractive blonde lady in a sleeveless pastel pink dress arrived at their table. She looked no older than thirty, Lottie estimated she was about twenty years younger than her husband.

'I was waiting for you in our room,' she said.

'Yes, I was on my way back when we were waylaid here by Mrs de Vere. Come and take a seat. Lemonade?'

'Yes please.'

Lord Harbottle introduced Mrs Moore to his wife.

'I hear you've just been on a trip to Luxor,' said Mrs Moore.

'Yes, we visited Tutankhamun's tomb.'

'Goodness! What's it like?'

'Well, it's dark inside and terribly old. And it's surrounded by desert which is so dreadfully hot and dusty.'

'I must admit, I don't fully understand who Tutankhamun was,' said Mrs Moore. 'Was he an important pharaoh?'

'Not terribly important,' said Mr Villiers. 'He ruled during the 18th dynasty, about three thousand years ago. He ascended the throne when he was about nine years old and died ten years later.'

'Golly, he was only nineteen? That's the same age as you, Lottie.'

'It's quite something to visit his tomb,' said Lord Harbottle. 'As soon as I heard about Carnarvon and Carter opening it last year, I knew I had to see it with my own eyes.'

'What did you make of it?'

'It's dark and old, as my good wife has said.'

'You wouldn't find me going in it,' said Mrs de Vere. 'Not with Lord Carnarvon's death a few weeks ago from the Pharaoh's Curse.'

Lottie gave a shiver. She'd read about Lord Carnarvon's death and the Pharoah's Curse in the newspapers.

'The curse is a load of old poppycock,' said Lord Harbottle.

'It is not! His death was sudden, and he was only fifty-six,' said Mrs de Vere. 'The curse is inscribed on the interior of the tomb. "Death shall come on swift wings to him who disturbs the peace of the King." I've read all about it.'

'How horrible!' said Mrs Moore.

'Lord Carnarvon's death was caused by an infected mosquito bite,' said Mr Villiers. 'Nothing to do with a curse.'

Mrs de Vere turned to Mrs Moore. 'Do you know that when Lord Carnarvon died at the Grand Continental Hotel here in Cairo, all the lights in the city went out? And a few hours later in England, his poor dog gave out a howl and died.'

'Oh no!' said Mrs Moore. 'How awful!'

'And possibly untrue,' said Mr Villiers.

'How many times have you visited the tomb, Mr Villiers?' asked Mrs de Vere.

'Five times.'

'Then you are five times more likely to be a victim of the Pharaoh's Curse!'

'What piffle. And even if there were such a thing as the Pharaoh's Curse, it can't affect me because I wear this around my neck.' He pulled out a little gold chain from beneath his collar. The chain had a small cross on it. 'It belonged to my mother, and it protects me.'

'But I went into the tomb and I wasn't wearing a cross!' said Lady Harbottle. 'Does that mean I'm cursed?'

'No darling, there's no such thing as the Pharaoh's Curse,'

said her husband. 'A good many men have visited that tomb since it was opened—'

'And ladies.'

'And ladies. And they're all walking about alive and well. The Pharaoh's Curse makes a good story, I grant you that, but there's no truth in it whatsoever.'

'So why does Benjamin wear a cross?' asked his wife.

'Just in case.'

'Just in case there is a curse? So that means there's a possibility?'

'I should say so,' said Mrs de Vere. 'After all, it's inscribed on the wall of the tomb.'

'The inscription doesn't exist,' said Mr Villiers. 'I've never seen it.'

'Perhaps we could change the topic?' suggested Mrs Moore.

'An excellent idea!' said Lord Harbottle. 'What a sensible lady you are, Mrs Moore. No more talk of silly superstitions.'

'I would be careful about what you dismiss as a silly superstition, Lord Harbottle,' said Mrs de Vere. 'Your words may come back to haunt you.'

THE LOBBY of Shepheard's Hotel had thick granite columns in the style of an ancient Egyptian temple. Copper lattice lamps hung on long chains and the tiled floor was covered with an enormous Persian rug.

Lottie and Rosie followed Mrs Moore to the reception desk where a suited man in a fez hat greeted them.

'Could you please deliver a message to Prince Manfred from me?' Mrs Moore asked.

'I'm afraid that will not be possible at the present time.'

'Why not?'

'We are under strict instructions that he is left undisturbed by fellow guests.'

'Oh dear. Is that so? I am quite well acquainted with the prince and I consider myself to be more than a mere fellow guest.'

'I understand, but we must respect his wishes.'

'Of course. May I ask what ails him?'

'I don't know the nature of his illness, but I understand a doctor is in regular attendance and that the prince is comfortable and in good spirits.'

'That's a relief to hear. I can imagine he's always in good spirits, whether in sickness or in health. I shall ask for regular updates on his progress if that's alright with you? I travelled to Cairo from Paris to meet with him and I do hope I can see him soon.'

'Of course.' The receptionist smiled and gave a polite bow.

'THERE's nothing more I can do, is there?' said Mrs Moore as they left the lobby and passed beneath an oversized arch edged in blue and white. They entered a lounge area with low leather seating and elaborately tiled walls.

'By the sound of things, the prince is being well looked after,' said Lottie.

'That's what the receptionist says, but we can't be sure, can we? If only I knew which suite he was in, then I could perhaps pay him a little visit.'

'The prince's staff says he must be left alone.'

'I realise that. But that just applies to the other guests, doesn't it? Few people here know him as well as I do. We were guests of his at the art exhibition in Paris, weren't we?'

'Along with a few hundred other people.'

'Yes, but we received a personal invitation. And we sat at a table close to his at that Paris restaurant. And he gifted us with dessert two nights in a row! Now there can't be many people in this hotel who can lay claim to that! We need to keep an eye out for a member of his entourage so I can pass on my good wishes. Oh poor Manfred, what if it's something serious? He could have gone down with an obscure tropical disease. And what if it's untreatable? I'm filled with worry now, Lottie.'

'The prince strikes me as a fit and healthy man. I'm sure he'll pull through.'

'Thank you, Lottie, that's what I like to think. Hopefully, it won't be too long before we receive news of his recovery.

Now, how about we take a little stroll before dinner? Hopefully, it will cool down soon and I've heard the Ezbekiya Garden is quite pretty.'

IT WAS a short walk to the garden from the hotel. The air was sultry, gritty, and not entirely fragrant. The buildings were tall, with shuttered windows and ornate wooden balconies. Intricate minaret towers rose above the rooftops. The pavement was busy with people browsing shops and stalls beneath tatty awnings. Oranges were piled high outside a fruit shop and bananas hung from hooks. Robed vendors attempted to draw attention to their wares: shoes, pots, hats, colourful quilts and paintings of Egyptian scenes. In the road, motor cars vied with donkey carts and a tram trundled through, sounding its bell.

Mrs Moore carried her parasol in one hand and her lorgnette in the other. 'Keep Rosie on her lead, Lottie, we don't want her dashing off like she did in Paris.'

Ezbekiya Garden provided some respite from the noise of the street. They found a path which took them around a small lake with swans bobbing on the water. Broadleaf trees and palm trees towered over spiky leaved agave plants.

'It's an interesting place, isn't it?' said Mrs Moore, peering through her lorgnette. 'Some of it reminds me of home and some of it feels completely different. I'd say it's where east meets west. And probably where south meets north too.'

A man approached, he wore a long blue robe and countless beaded necklaces around his neck. More necklaces dangled from each arm.

'Cheap price.' He grinned at them.

'Oh no, a street hawker,' said Mrs Moore.

'Cheap price.'

'No thank you.'

'Cheap price.'

'Shall we head back to the hotel, Lottie?'

'Cheap price!' he called after them.

ANOTHER STREET HAWKER was selling necklaces close to the hotel, he stood next to his stall in the shade of a gnarled tree. He was a young man in a waistcoat and white trousers, and he wore a white cap on his head. Rosie immediately warmed to him and pulled Lottie in his direction.

'Don't go near the street hawker!' said Mrs Moore. 'We've only just escaped one!'

Lottie tried pulling Rosie back, but the dog was very insistent. The young man smiled at them both. Lottie had never seen her dog so interested in someone before, she thought it best to allow Rosie to greet him. He stooped to pat the dog's head and Rosie wagged her tail. Lottie prepared herself to refuse him when he tried to sell her a necklace.

'Your dog is very friendly,' he said.

'You speak English?'

'Yes, and some French, too. What's your dog's name?'

'Rosie.'

'Are you staying at Shepheard's Hotel?'

'Yes.'

'My brother works in the kitchen there. If you see him say hello, his name is Ahmed.'

'I'll look out for him.'

He gave her a handsome smile. 'I hope you enjoy your stay.'

'Thank you.' There was something about his dark eyes which made Lottie blush a little.

'Have you told him you're not buying anything?' called out Mrs Moore.

'Yes.'

'You're not buying anything?' he said. 'Now my heart is broken.'

'I'm sure it's not really,' said Lottie with a giggle.

'It was very nice to meet you and Rosie.'

'Come along, Lottie!' said Mrs Moore. 'Don't let him charm you.'

Chapter Four

AFTER DRESSING FOR DINNER, Mrs Moore chose a spot in the lounge where she and Lottie could relax with a drink. Their seat had a clear view of the lobby and the walkway through to the garden at the rear of hotel.

'If any of Prince Manfred's chaps stroll through here, I'll spot them immediately,' said Mrs Moore, looking through her lorgnette.

Rosie rested by Lottie's feet, enjoying the coolness of the tiled floor.

A grinning, suntanned man in a smart suit approached.

'Mr Villiers!' said Mrs Moore.

'Mind if I join you?'

'Not at all.'

He pulled up a rattan chair, placed some books on the table and sat down.

'Some reading material, Mr Villiers?'

'Absolutely.' He gave a proud smile. 'We have here *Egyptian Temples*, *A Concise Dictionary of Egyptian Archae-ology* and *The Life and Times of Akhenaten*.'

'Gosh.'

'I'm always learning. It's an important part of the job for us archaeologists. It's not enormously well paid though which is why I also earn a few bob taking people to King Tut's tomb, this hotel is perfect for picking up business. I have to say that I adore Cairo, I don't believe there's a place quite like it, is there? It's a marvellous mix of the Arab world and the European world. The British have done an excellent job of looking after this country.'

'I have to say that the recent history of Egypt confuses me a little,' said Mrs Moore.

'It is confusing. Cigarette?'

'No, thank you. But I don't mind if you smoke, Mr Villiers.'

'Thank you.' He lit his cigarette and puffed out a cloud of smoke. 'Well Egypt was part of the Ottoman Empire for a bit, then Napoleon moved in, then the British moved in and moved Napoleon out. And then... yes it's quite confusing. That was about a hundred and twenty years ago. Then I think it was the Ottomans again for a bit... then the British came back. There was a revolution here just after the war because Egypt wanted to rule itself.'

'I can understand that.'

'But the British are still here, even though Egyptian independence was declared last year. It's probably something to do with the Suez Canal which is an important trade route between the Mediterranean and the Red Sea, I think the British want to keep control of it.'

'I don't see why.'

'I put it down to politics, Mrs Moore. And I have to say that politics bores me.' He exhaled another cloud of smoke. 'In the meantime, Egypt is a fabulous playground, wouldn't you say?'

'I hadn't quite considered it like that. How long have you been out here?'

'I've been in the Middle East for about three months, I've worked on digs in Mesopotamia and Syria but Egypt is my favourite.'

'And who are your family?'

He pulled a grimace. 'Not landed gentry, if that's what you're hoping. My father runs a chain of furniture shops.'

'There's no shame in that, Mr Villiers,' said Mrs Moore. 'My father was a successful railroad tycoon in Pennsylvania and yet he was born in a shepherd's bothy in Scotland.'

'Good heavens, what's that?'

'A little hut which shepherds shelter in on Scottish hillsides.'

'So your father was Scottish?'

'Yes.'

'Lovely place Scotland. So I've heard. I've never actually been there. Probably because it's full of Scots!' He laughed at his joke.

'Some of them are my family,' said Mrs Moore stiffly.

'Ah yes.' He recovered himself. 'I suppose they would be. It was just a little quip of mine, I like Scottish people very much. So what are you hoping to see here in Cairo, Mrs Moore?'

'Some pyramids would be nice. I'm not sure what else there is, to be honest with you. Where do you recommend?'

'The pyramids of Giza should be at the top of your list and don't forget you can see the Sphinx there too. Then you should visit Al-Azhar Mosque, the Citadel, the Khan el-Khalili bazaar, the Egyptian Museum and the Coptic Museum.'

'I don't think I can remember all those.'

'Let me write them down for you.'

He stubbed out his cigarette and took a pen and notebook from his jacket pocket. He wrote down the sights then ripped out the piece of paper and handed it to Mrs Moore. 'There you go. Now there's no excuse for not visiting any of them. Do you see what I've also written on there?'

'Luxor and the Valley of the Kings.'

'That's right, that's the tour I've just taken the Harbottles on!' He chuckled. 'Rather cheeky of me to include that, but I beg you to consider it. The trip takes about five days and is worth every penny. Give it some thought, Mrs Moore. Oh look who it is! Mrs de Vere!' He waved to the old lady in black who was slowly approaching them with the aid of her walking stick.

'How wonderful,' said Mrs Moore. Lottie noticed her voice lacked enthusiasm.

'Good evening,' said the old lady, resting her walking stick against the table and slowly making herself comfortable. Jewels sparkled at her neck and wrists. 'You're still here then, Mr Villiers?' she said.

'Yes. Why wouldn't I be?'

'Not dropped dead from the Pharaoh's Curse yet, then?'

His face reddened. 'Not only has that joke worn thin, Mrs de Vere, it wasn't particularly funny in the first place.'

The old lady laughed. 'I only say it to annoy you.'

'I realise that.' He lit another cigarette. 'Do excuse me, but I've arranged to meet a friend in the bar.'

Mrs de Vere chuckled as he walked away. 'He's absolutely terrified by that curse.'

'Terrified?' said Mrs Moore.

'Yes. We already know about the cross he wears to protect himself and I should think he lies awake at night worrying that he's going to come down with a deadly illness because he's stepped into Tutankhamun's tomb five times.'

'But if it bothers him so much, then why does he go there?'

'Because he makes money from his trips to the Valley of the Kings. I don't know exactly how much the Harbottles paid him, but it would have been a small fortune, I'm sure of it. It seems the young man can't take my jokes, he got quite irate with me the other day about it. He needs to be careful how he speaks to me though, I could make a lot of trouble for him.'

'Could you?'

The old lady narrowed her lizard-like eyes. 'Yes, I could simply advise guests here not to go on his tours. I know they'd listen to me and he would lose out, wouldn't he?'

'I'm sure that would be quite unnecessary. Perhaps it's time to stop joking about the Pharaoh's Curse?'

'Perhaps it is. But the trouble is, I have so much fun with it. Waiter!' She ordered a gin and tonic, then turned to Mrs Moore. 'Any sign of the Harbottles yet?'

'Not yet.'

'Perhaps Lord Harbottle has received another telephone call about one of his children. He was late to dinner the other evening for that reason.'

'What happened?'

'Surely you must have heard all about Lord Harbottle's children?'

'No.'

'He has three children with his first wife. The current Lady Harbottle is his second wife, there are a few stories I can tell you about her.'

'Really?'

'Yes. But as for the children, poor Lord Harbottle has spent the past twenty years trying to keep them in line. I think he's practically given up now.'

'What's wrong with the Harbottle children?'

'Well, first, there's Edward. He holds the honour of having been expelled from both Eton and Harrow. In the end, they had to send him to a boarding school in Devon in the middle of Dartmoor. Somehow, he escaped and was caught trying to steal a boat in Exmouth to get across the channel to France. Oxford University didn't want him and neither did Cambridge, so he was sent off to the army. You'd have thought that would have sorted him out, wouldn't you? But even the army didn't want him and somehow they got him into the navy. The last I heard, he was on a boat in the South China Sea. Probably the best place for him, if you ask me.'

'And the other children?'

'Matilda. She's quite wild and is a dancer in London, despite an expensive formal education. She's very beautiful and was married to a trumpet player for fifteen days. She's quite scandalised the family name, as you can imagine. Poor Lord Harbottle had to take to his bed for three weeks when he learned of Matilda's disastrous marriage.'

'Actually longer than she was married for.'

'Exactly. I think he's washing his hands of her now. There was a time when he had to keep going to London to fetch her home, but I fear her reputation is quite ruined now. And the youngest is Bertrand and fancies himself as a bit of a dandy. He's at Oxford, so he's fared a little better than his brother, but apparently he spends little time on his studies and prefers to press flowers and write poetry.'

'That sounds like a pleasant way to pass one's time.'

'Not if he's to be the heir. I should think Edward will be disinherited and Bertrand will inherit the family's estate. Apparently he's told his parents that he has no intention of ever marrying. What a thing to say! No consideration at all for the family. At this rate, there will be no Harbottle heirs at all. Not unless the second Lady Harbottle produces one, but time must be running out for her now and she doesn't strike me as the maternal type. Lord Harbottle has brought it all on himself.'

'Why do you say that?'

Mrs de Vere lowered her voice. 'He spoiled them. He

spared the rod and ruined the child, as they say. The first Lady Harbottle was too involved in their lives when she should have left the duties to nannies and governesses. Such people are well-trained and know what they're doing. But instead, Lord and Lady Harbottle spoiled the children and now they're unable to manage themselves as adults. I'm not a parent myself, but it's easy to see where it all went wrong. I think Lord Harbottle does a marvellous job of pretending everything is normal. It's quite amazing how few people know about his delinquent offspring, I was discussing this with some people here yesterday and they had no idea!' The old lady paused to sip her gin, then continued. 'You do realise that the second Lady Harbottle was an actress?'

'No.'

'Her name was Polly Higgins.' She gave a dry laugh. 'Rather ordinary, wouldn't you say? Apparently, he saw her in a performance of *Lady Windermere's Fan* and he was smitten. Left his first wife immediately. Before that, Polly Higgins was famous for having an affair with Sir George Efford.'

'Who's he?'

'You've not heard of him?'

'No.'

'He was a cabinet secretary or something. Someone important in the government. I forgot you're an American, so I suppose you wouldn't have any interest in British politics. It was quite a scandal at the time and Polly was named in the divorce case. She put an end to Sir George's marriage, then did the same with Lord Harbottle's marriage! She's not particularly liked in London society. However, I've always found her quite pleasant, and she does well for a lady who wasn't born into the position she now holds. Have you seen something, Mrs Moore?'

'A member of Prince Manfred's entourage, I think.' Mrs Moore had clearly grown bored with the conversation and was peering through her lorgnette at someone in the lobby. 'I want to find out if the prince is recovering alright.'

'I'm sure he is. You can't imagine a proud man like him going down without a fight. He thinks very highly of himself.'

'Because he's royalty.'

'I suppose that could be something to do with it. Only Bavarian royalty though, the family barely features on the world stage since his father's abdication. And I've heard the prince is little more than an overgrown child.'

Mrs Moore lowered her lorgnette. 'I beg your pardon?'

'Apparently, he's been terribly spoiled since the day he was born and is incapable of tying his own shoelaces or combing his hair.'

'Where did you hear such nonsense?'

'It's to be expected, I suppose. When you're born into royalty, you have countless people doing all these things for you. One need never do anything for oneself.'

'Prince Manfred is quite capable of tying his shoelaces!'

'Do you know that for sure?'

'He must be, the man is fifty years old! And it must be difficult being a gentleman in his position because people can be such dreadful gossips and spreaders of false rumour. I refuse to believe any of that garbage.'

'Very well. That's your choice, Mrs Moore. It's only natural you wouldn't wish to hear him being spoken of in unflattering terms. I merely pass on information which I hear from reliable sources.'

LOTTIE AND MRS MOORE dined with Lord and Lady Harbottle that evening. The hotel restaurant was furnished with ornate mirrors, decorative wall tiles and glossy leaved plants in shiny copper pots. Lottie had been expecting Egyptian food but discovered everything on the menu was French. She was happy with this, having enjoyed the food in Paris.

Mrs de Vere sat with a grey-haired lady in purple at another table, Lottie felt relieved they didn't have to endure the old lady's gossip and opinions for the rest of the evening. Mrs Moore's mood had cooled since Mrs de Vere had described Prince Manfred as an overgrown child.

'Where's that marvellous dog of yours?' Lord Harbottle asked her.

'Under my chair,' said Lottie.

'Under your chair? The dog needs a chair of her own!' He clicked his fingers at a waiter and a short while later, Rosie had her own chair and place setting. Her little face just reached above the table.

'Now what will she have to eat?' Lord Harbottle asked.

25

'You're such a silly billy, Bartholomew,' said his wife. She had dressed for the occasion in a carnation pink dress and a diaphanous cape trimmed with ostrich feathers.

'Better a silly billy than a down-in-the-mouth,' said Lord Harbottle.

'I'm not a down-in-the-mouth!'

'Did I call you a down-in-the-mouth?'

'Not in so many words.'

'I didn't call you one, so there. Villiers!' He waved to the archaeologist who stood grinning in the restaurant doorway. 'Who's he with?'

'Hugo Whitaker,' said Lady Harbottle with a smile.

'Who's he?'

'He runs tours. I met him earlier this afternoon.'

'Why wasn't I there?' asked Lord Harbottle.

'You were obviously doing something else, darling.'

The two men sat at a neighbouring table, and Mr Villiers introduced his companion. Mr Whitaker was in his forties and had a handsome, rectangular face. His grey hair was neatly trimmed and his blue eyes had a sparkle to them. 'I like to see a dog being well looked after.' He nodded at Rosie. 'What's he having for dinner?'

'He is a she,' corrected Mrs Moore. 'And it's lovely to meet you, Mr Whitaker. Are you staying long in Cairo?'

'This place is my home now. I came here during the war and have stayed here ever since.'

'How come I haven't met you yet?' asked Lord Harbottle.

'Mr Whitaker had an unfortunate habit of hanging out at the Grand Continental Hotel,' said Mr Villiers. 'I've persuaded him to join us here at Shepheard's instead.'

'You came out here with the army, Mr Whitaker?' asked Mrs Moore.

'I did indeed. And now I organise itineraries for tourists to see the sights of Egypt. I adore every moment.'

'How marvellous.'

'There are a few spaces left on tomorrow's excursion on camelback to the pyramids if anyone would like to join us. I've already asked Lady Harbottle.'

'Yes, you have,' she replied. Lottie noticed her gaze was fixed on him. 'And I'd like to go!'

'To the pyramids, Polly?' said her husband. 'We've already been!'

'But we can go again!'

'Why? There's nothing else to see there. All that's there are three big pyramids, a few tumbledown little ones, a sphinx and some tombs and a lot of old stones. And besides, I've made other plans for us tomorrow.'

'Such as what?'

'The races at Gezira Park.'

'I suppose that's quite appealing, I do enjoy the races.'

'I know you do, that's why I arranged it. I'm sorry we can't make it tomorrow, Mr Whitaker.'

'Do you enjoy the races back home, Lady Harbottle?' asked Mr Whitaker.

'I do indeed! The Epsom Derby is my favourite.'

'The Epsom Derby is also my favourite.'

'Is it?'

'Oh yes, I'm there most years. I usually go back to England in the summer because it's too hot here, the Epsom Derby fits into my social calendar perfectly.'

'Well, that is wonderful,' said Lady Harbottle with a broad smile. 'We'll probably see you there this summer then!'

'I'm sure you will.'

'I shall look forward to it!'

'Me too, Lady Harbottle.'

Lord Harbottle's moustache twitched with irritation. 'Where have the waiters got to?' he snapped. 'A man could easily die in here of thirst and hunger before anyone notices.'

'Fancy the Turf Club this evening, Harbottle?' said Mr Villiers.

'Yes, why not?'

'Really Bartholomew?' said Lady Harbottle. 'You were there until late last night.'

'It will only be for a few games of cards. What time shall we leave, Villiers?'

'Half past nine? Or earlier if you fancy a little spin beforehand.'

'You have a car do you?' asked Mrs Moore.

'Better than that, it's a motorcycle.' He grinned. 'And it has a sidecar too. I just stick old Harbottle in the sidecar and off we go.'

Lottie couldn't help noticing Lady Harbottle's thunderous expression.

AFTER DINNER, Lottie, Mrs Moore and Rosie sat on the terrace. The evening air was balmy, and the terrace was lit with flickering lanterns. Crickets chirruped from somewhere close by.

'I had a little wander around the hotel earlier,' said Mrs Moore. 'And I think I know which room Prince Manfred is in. There appears to be a large suite on the third floor and I'm sure I overheard people speaking German when I walked past. I think I've done quite well to track him down, there are three hundred and forty bedrooms in this place. Isn't that astonishing? One of the receptionists told me that.'

'Mind if I join you?' said Mrs de Vere, sinking herself into a wicker chair. 'Lovely evening, isn't it?'

'It is,' said Mrs Moore, picking up her lorgnette. 'Is that Mr Villiers over there? I thought he was going for a spin with Lord Harbottle.'

'Where?' The old lady resembled a tortoise as she craned her head. 'Oh, over there! I see him now.'

Mr Villiers stood on the terrace talking with a glamorous Arab lady, the pair were laughing together.

'Who's he talking to?' asked Mrs Moore.

'Mayar Omar,' said Mrs de Vere. 'She owns a nightclub.'

'Owns it?'

'Yes, she's done very well for herself. It's not the sort of place which you or I would set foot in, Mrs Moore. It's quite disreputable. A lot of tawdry dancing and singing. The gentlemen seem to like it and I think it's obvious why.' She wrinkled her nose. 'It wouldn't surprise me if Villiers frequents Miss Omar's club. I don't understand why they allow her into this hotel.'

'Why not?'

'Because she comes here touting for business. Look at how she charms Villiers! He can't wipe that silly grin off his face, can he? She must make a fortune from all the gentlemen.'

'I suppose she knows what she's doing.'

Lottie watched as the pair strolled into the hotel together.

'Oh yes,' said Mrs de Vere. 'She knows what she's doing alright. She'll be perfectly pleasant to you, Mrs Moore, but I'm afraid she's the sort of lady who's only interested in speaking to members of the opposite sex. It's quite impossible to have a friendship with her, I should know because I tried. What a waste of time that was.'

'What happened?'

'She befriended me during her regular visits to this hotel and I'm a very welcoming person, as you know. She's an excellent conversationalist, she speaks five languages, and I regret to say she's very intelligent too. So we had a great deal in common.'

'You speak five languages?'

'No, I meant the intelligent part. I can see why she was

drawn to me, because I know everyone. But I wasted my energies on her, she was only using me for introductions to gentlemen to invite to her club. She wasn't interested in me at all! It's disappointing when someone befriends you only for your reputation. I usually sniff those types out quickly, but I was caught out this time round.'

'What did she do?'

'She no longer wished to have anything to do with me.'

'She told you that?'

'No, but I noticed that when she came to the hotel, my table was no longer the first she visited. She got what she could from me and didn't want to know me after that. Some people are extremely superficial.'

'I'm sorry to hear it, Mrs de Vere, it sounds as though you're better off without her.'

'I am, aren't I? She's only successful because she's so beautiful. However, she'll grow old and ugly like the rest of us and then where will she be?'

Mrs Moore stifled a yawn and announced she was going to retire for the evening. Lottie felt pleased with this, she struggled to enjoy Mrs de Vere's company. It seemed the old lady didn't have anything nice to say about anybody.

LOTTIE FOLLOWED Mrs Moore to the main staircase. As they ascended, Rosie had other ideas and trotted off down a corridor.

'Rosie!' Lottie called after her, but the dog didn't respond.

'Oh dear,' said Mrs Moore. 'Do you need my help to fetch her?'

'No, it's fine, you go on up and I'll get her,' said Lottie.

As she went after Rosie, she could hear a hum of voices growing louder. The dog turned a corner and Lottie followed to find herself in the doorway of a bar. Rosie had clearly been drawn to the excitable chatter, and she rapidly disappeared between the legs of the drinkers.

Lottie sighed. All she could do was fight her way through the throng to find her. Strains of piano music floated from a corner of the room.

'Miss Sprigg!' She turned to see Benjamin Villiers and Hugo Whitaker. 'Joining us for a drink?'

'That's kind of you, but no thank you, I came in here to find my dog. She ran away from me.'

'That lovely little corgi? How naughty! We can help look for her.'

The two men helped Lottie search for Rosie. It wasn't easy in the crowded bar. Lottie threaded her way past men in suits and military uniform and ladies in colourful evening gowns. The longer she searched, the more she worried. Perhaps Rosie had left the bar and gone elsewhere? Had she gone outside and wandered down the street? Lottie tried not to imagine the worst.

Laughter sounded behind her, then she felt something cold and wet on her back.

A spilt drink.

'William!' said a woman's voice behind her. 'You apologise to that young lady at once!'

Lottie turned to see Mayar Omar looking at her with concern. 'Are you alright?' she asked Lottie.

'I'm fine.'

'I'm dreadfully sorry,' flustered a chubby man in a striped suit. 'Harry knocked into me.'

'No, he didn't,' said Miss Omar. 'You're just trying to blame someone else for your clumsiness. Now be a gentleman and take responsibility for your mistake.'

He apologised to Lottie again. 'I'll happily pay for your dress to be laundered,' he said.

'Is that all?' asked Miss Omar.

'What else can I do?'

'How about arranging for a bouquet of flowers to be delivered to the young lady's room?'

'That's really not necessary,' said Lottie, keen to resume her search for Rosie.

'Yes it is,' said Miss Omar. 'We all like a bouquet of flowers, don't we?' She addressed William. 'And you can buy me a bouquet too.'

'Why?'

'Because you're a gentleman.' She turned back to Lottie. 'You're the American heiress's assistant, aren't you?'

'Yes, how did you know?'

'You were both pointed out to me earlier. Don't look so worried!' She laughed. 'No one goes unnoticed here at Shepheard's Hotel.'

Lottie smiled. 'I don't suppose you've seen my dog, have you? She's a Welsh Pembroke Corgi.'

'Now you come to mention it, we have. We saw a dog here a few minutes ago and wondered what it was up to.'

'She went that way,' said William, pointing to a far wall. 'And I'm sorry again about your dress.'

Lottie walked on in the direction William had indicated, her wet dress clinging to her back. She felt annoyed at Rosie for running off, yet concerned at the same time. What if she never saw her again?

Her fears evaporated as soon as she saw Mr Villiers cradling Rosie in his arms. 'I found her under the piano,' he said. 'She looked like she was regretting her decision to come into this noisy place. Here you are.' He handed the dog back to Lottie. 'You're lucky I was here, I'm just about to go out with old Harbottle.'

'Thank you so much!'

'Don't mention it. And what better cause for celebration

than Hugo Whitaker offering you and Mrs Moore a discount on his trip to the pyramids on camelback!'

'What?' said Mr Whitaker.

'Come on Hugo, be a sport.'

'Alright then.'

'Good, that's settled.'

'I'd better check with Mrs Moore before I agree to anything,' said Lottie.

'Of course. I'm sure she'll agree to it though,' said Mr Villiers. 'All the ladies like handsome Hugo!' He gave his friend a pat on the back and Lottie chose the moment to make her excuses and leave.

Chapter Six

Lottie wearily climbed the staircase with Rosie in her arms. 'I suppose your escape wasn't completely in vain,' she said to her dog. 'We managed to arrange a discounted trip to the pyramids. I can't wait to see them! I can only hope Mrs Moore agrees to it.'

As she reached the corridor on the next floor, Lottie saw a dark figure approaching.

Mrs de Vere.

Instinctively, she ducked behind one of the large granite columns at the top of the staircase. She knew it was rude, but she couldn't face another conversation with the sharp-tongued old lady.

She held onto Rosie and waited for Mrs de Vere to pass. But she didn't. And a moment later, Lottie heard another voice.

'I'd like to politely request that you keep your mouth shut, Mrs de Vere.' It sounded like Lady Harbottle.

'I beg your pardon?'

'Lord Harbottle has just had to endure a third person

offering him their sympathies on the supposed waywardness
of his children.'

'Well, that was nice of them.'

'I don't think it was nice at all, I think they only brought
the topic up because they were hoping to hear more salacious
stories. Stories which you told them.'

'Me?'

'Lord Harbottle's children are his own concern, not yours,
Mrs de Vere. You have no right to go about the place telling
people about our supposed family woes. My husband is excep-
tionally proud of his three children and we don't need you
spreading harmful rumours and giving our family a bad name.'

'Well I'm sorry if the truth offends you, Lady Harbottle.'

'*Truth*? There is no truth in what you're telling people. I
don't deny that the Harbottle children have made a few slip-
ups in their time, but their lives are not your business. Neither
is the nonsense you tell people about Sir George Efford.'

'You can't pretend such scandal didn't happen, Lady
Harbottle. Or Polly Higgins as you were then.'

'That's enough! If I hear again that you've been spreading
rumours about our family then—'

'Then what, Lady Harbottle?'

'I'm politely asking you to stop gossiping about our
family. I'm surprised that a lady of your class and background
stoops so low as to spread tittle-tattle about others. I can only
imagine you have nothing else interesting to talk about in your
conversations, what a terrible shame that is. It must be rather
sad leading a life that's so dull and uneventful that the only
interesting topic of conversation is the affairs of other people.'

'You flatter yourself that I'm even interested in the affairs
of someone like you, Lady Harbottle. And my conversation is
intelligent and wide-ranging.'

Lady Harbottle laughed.

'The Harbottle family has a high profile,' continued Mrs de Vere. 'And people are therefore interested in the children. After all, they will continue the Harbottle family name. I never gossip, I merely pass on nuggets of information which I learn from my wide social circle.'

'I call that gossip, Mrs de Vere, and I won't hear any more excuses for why you feel the need to indulge in it. I've already told you what I think of the manner in which you conduct yourself, and I suggest you come up with new topics of conversation. Lots of people consider you a terrible gossip, not just me.'

'Nonsense, I know I'm highly thought of here.'

'Do you live in a hotel in Cairo because you were excluded from polite society back home? Perhaps that's the real reason you're here?'

'You can be very spiteful, Lady Harbottle, but I refuse to be riled by it.'

'Let my words serve as a warning to you, if I hear you've been gossiping about our family again... I shall have to do something about it.'

'Then do so, Lady Harbottle. It will be interesting to see what you're capable of.'

Chapter Seven

A BOUQUET of flowers was delivered to Lottie's room the following morning.

'You have an admirer already, Lottie?' said Mrs Moore when she showed them to her.

'No, they're from someone who spilt a drink on my dress while I was looking for Rosie in the bar last night. There was no need for him to send them.'

'Well I think they're very pretty. Now come on, let's hope they're still serving breakfast. We're rather late this morning, aren't we? All that travelling has caught up with me. Or maybe it's the heat? It's probably both. Who knows?'

As they descended the main staircase, Lottie told her employer about the discount Mr Whitaker was offering on his trip to the pyramids. 'Do you think we could go today?' Lottie asked.

'Riding on a camel?'

'Yes!' Lottie was excited about the idea.

'I'll have to think about it.'

'But you want to see the pyramids, don't you?'

'I'm quite happy to observe them from a shady veranda

with a glass of lemonade in my hand. Or from the seat of a motor car with someone driving me about. I'm unsure about a camel, though.'

'You can't visit Egypt without riding on a camel, Mrs Moore.'

Her employer laughed. 'I suppose not, I like your enthusiasm, Lottie. I'll have a think about it.'

They reached the lobby and saw a group of police officers in buttoned jackets, breeches and long boots.

'Odd,' said Mrs Moore. 'Let's get some breakfast.'

But the hotel restaurant was closed.

'I'm extremely sorry, madam, but there has been an incident,' said a waiter.

'What sort of incident?'

'A guest has been taken unwell.'

'So you've closed the entire restaurant? What about my breakfast?'

'I apologise for that, madam. We can serve you with some food in the lounge.'

'Very well. Oh my goodness, it's not Prince Manfred, is it?'

'What do you mean, madam?'

'In there.' Mrs Moore pointed at the closed restaurant door. 'He's not the guest who's been taken unwell?'

'No, madam.'

'Thank goodness for that.' They walked on to the lounge. 'I'm relieved to hear that, Lottie. I thought, for one horrible moment, that Prince Manfred had thought himself recovered enough for breakfast this morning, then had a funny turn in the restaurant.'

There was barely room to sit in the lounge and guests talked in hushed tones. Mrs Moore found a seat and scanned the room through her lorgnette. 'Mr Villiers is over there talking to a police officer,' she said. 'He looks dreadfully serious. Let's grab him as soon as he's finished.'

A few moments later, Mrs Moore found her opportunity.

'It's Mrs de Vere,' he said with tears in his eyes. 'The policeman has just told me she's dead!'

Mrs Moore gasped. 'Dead?'

'Dead!'

'How?'

'I don't know! One moment I was speaking to her and then the next...'

'You were with her?'

'Yes, we were having breakfast together. I really don't understand it, perhaps her heart gave out or something.'

'But that's so sad.'

'It is, I can't believe it. All the staff were very good, and the waiters came to help. There's a doctor staying here at the hotel and he did all he could. Are you alright Mrs Moore? You look a little pale.'

'I think I'm in shock.'

'Tea with plenty of sugar, that's what you need.'

'Yes, I think I do.'

'I'll find a waiter for you.'

'Gosh, Lottie,' said Mrs Moore. 'I don't understand it at all. I realise Mrs de Vere wasn't young, but her health seemed good, didn't it? She seemed in fine shape for a lady of her age. Perhaps she was nursing an ailment which we didn't realise?'

Lady Harbottle joined them, she was pale and her eyes were rimmed with red. 'It's so awfully sad, I'm going to miss her enormously. It couldn't have happened to a nicer lady. She made my husband and me feel extremely welcome here in Cairo, and it's an absolute travesty.'

Lottie was struck by the difference between these words and the ones Lady Harbottle had said to Mrs de Vere during their altercation the previous evening.

'It's awful indeed,' said Mrs Moore. 'I suppose someone

must have informed her family back home. What family does she have?'

'I'm not sure. She didn't have children, and she had been widowed for many years.'

'But she had money?'

'She must have, she wore a lot of expensive looking jewellery, didn't she? And she told me and Bartholomew that her husband had come from a wealthy family.'

'I wonder who will inherit her fortune?'

'I don't know. Perhaps she's left it all to her maid?' Lady Harbottle let out a sob. 'It's all so sad!'

A waiter arrived with tea and Mrs Moore thanked him. 'I was all set for breakfast,' she said to Lady Harbottle. 'But I've quite lost my appetite now.'

'Me too.'

'You must join me in having some sugary tea, it will help with the shock.'

Lottie had some tea too and enjoyed its warmth and sweetness. Then she cuddled Rosie on her lap and watched the fellow guests discussing the tragic news. She hadn't liked Mrs de Vere very much, but her sudden death was upsetting all the same.

Lord Harbottle arrived. He helped himself to some tea, then addressed them, his voice low and serious. 'Don't go shouting about this,' he said. 'I don't want to cause any alarm. But I've just been speaking to a policeman who tells me they're suspecting poison.'

'Poison?' said his wife.

'Keep your voice down, Polly, this isn't common knowledge yet. But they've found suspicious residue at the bottom of Mrs de Vere's teacup. According to Villiers, she drank her tea, then pulled an odd face. Then she was peering into the cup before she fell ill.'

'Someone poisoned her?' said Mrs Moore.

'Indeed. Dreadful isn't it?' He smoothed his moustache. 'Poor Villiers has had a bit of questioning from the police because he was at the table with her at the time. But he says he didn't see anyone put anything in her tea. If you ask me, the poison was put in her drink before it was taken to her table.'

'One of the waiters?' said Mrs Moore.

'Could have been. But I don't see why a waiter would do such a thing. Unless it was someone she'd complained about. She liked to complain, didn't she?'

'Let's not speak ill of the dead. Bartholomew.'

'I'm sorry darling, but I'm just telling it like it is. The old dear clearly upset someone and they've done away with her.'

'Benjamin says he didn't see anyone put poison in her drink, but he could have done it himself,' said Lady Harbottle.

'Villiers wouldn't do such a thing! But there's no denying he had the opportunity, and that's why the poor fellow is having to explain himself to the police. It doesn't look good for him, does it?'

Lottie recalled Mrs de Vere taunting Mr Villiers about the Pharaoh's Curse. Could he really have taken such an objection to her words that he'd poisoned her? It seemed an overreaction.

'Anyway, the trouble is lots of people passed by Mrs de Vere's table at breakfast this morning,' said Lord Harbottle. 'You and I included, Polly.'

'Only briefly. We stopped and wished her and Benjamin good morning. I didn't see you put any poison in her tea and you didn't see me put any poison in her tea, so I think we're in the clear.'

'But we might have to explain ourselves to the police.'

'Why?'

'For that very reason you've just given, darling. We both stopped at her table.'

'And when we were eating breakfast, I saw Miss Omar stop and talk to Mr Villiers.'

'That's right! I recall that now. I remember thinking it was unusual to see Miss Omar in the hotel at breakfast time, she must have stayed here last night for some reason. Thinking about it, I think she's the one most likely to have poisoned Mrs de Vere.'

'Why?' asked Mrs Moore.

'She just strikes me as the sort.'

'Why does she strike you as the sort?' said his wife. 'You barely know her.'

'That's right, I barely know her. But I've been around long enough to know when someone's a bit shifty. Even if it's someone I barely know.'

'Are you judging her because of her line of work?' said Mrs Moore.

'I'd say she's a lady with loose morals,' said Lord Harbottle, and his wife nodded in agreement. 'So that's why I suspect her. Murdering someone is simply below the belt. Who on earth, in their right mind, would wish to harm a defenceless old lady? As soon as the culprit is caught, they should be hanged, drawn and quartered. No clemency should be shown whatsoever. Hopefully, the Egyptian authorities aren't as soft as they are back home with these matters. This sort of behaviour needs to be clamped down on and the perpetrator made an example of. It's a despicable act!'

'Perhaps it was a mistake?' suggested his wife.

'What do you mean?'

'Maybe the poison was intended for Benjamin instead?'

'Why would someone want to harm Villiers?'

'I don't know because I don't know what company he keeps. But he's a very successful archaeologist, perhaps he has a rival who envies his success? I should think that's the most likely reason.'

'It's a possibility, I suppose,' said Lord Harbottle. 'But why go about poisoning anybody in the first place? It's an extremely cowardly act. If I have a problem with a fellow, then I settle it like a proper gentleman, man-to-man. What's wrong with a good old-fashioned fistfight? Or a duel, for that matter. My grandfather managed all his affairs in duels. Until he was shot.'

'Oh goodness!' said Mrs Moore.

'He survived. He never got the sensation back in his left arm though, the bullet went right through the top of it. Like a hot knife through butter, according to my mother.'

'Bartholomew!' said Lady Harbottle. 'We don't want to hear about that!'

'But that's the way it was in those days. Everything was above board and there was none of this sneaking about putting poison into people's cups of tea. However did mankind sink to such depths?'

'I think these things have always gone on, Lord Harbottle,' said Mrs Moore. 'Even the ancient Egyptians probably poisoned each other.'

'But it wasn't an ancient Egyptian that poisoned Mrs de Vere, was it? It was somebody in this hotel while we were all enjoying a pleasant breakfast. And now we're all going to be too terrified to have breakfast each morning. It's a disgrace. And where did the chap get hold of poison, anyway? They need to find the man who sold it to him and ensure he pays with his life too.'

'Whoever sold it to him can't possibly have known that he was going to poison an old lady with it,' said Lady Harbottle.

'I should think it's quite obvious that someone buying poison is going to cause trouble with it. Poison is tricky to get hold of back home, and rightly so. But in other countries, like this one, the rules are rather lax. Before we know it, we could all be poisoned!'

'Oh Bartholomew! Don't say such things. It frightens me!'

'Murder is a frightening business, Polly, and we can't get complacent about it. We need to be on our guard until this man is caught. I'm going to offer the police my help in this matter.'

'By doing what?'

'Scouting around this hotel until I find the miscreant.'

'But how will you know who the poisoner is? He's not going to make himself obvious, is he?'

'No, he's not, but I've got a nose for these things. I may have been born into the wrong class to be a policeman, but if I'd become one, then I'd have been the best detective there ever was.'

Chapter Eight

'ARE those policemen staring at me, Lottie?' asked Mrs Moore.

Lottie watched the two men have a brief discussion, then approach.

'Yes,' she replied. 'It looks like they want to talk to you.'

'Me? Why? I wasn't even at breakfast when Mrs de Vere was poisoned!'

'You need to explain that to them, not me.'

'Mrs Moore?' said one of the policemen. He sounded British, his companion looked Egyptian.

'Yes, how do you know my name?' she said.

'May we speak with you a moment?'

'Yes. Why?'

'We shall explain.'

Lord Harbottle got to his feet. 'My wife and I will excuse ourselves so you have some privacy.'

As soon as the Harbottles had vacated their seats, the policemen sat down in them.

'Oh,' said Mrs Moore. 'I feel like I'm in trouble. Why? I've done nothing wrong!'

45

The British policeman took a notebook from his pocket.
'Name?'

'You know my name, you just addressed me by it.'

'I need your full name.'

'Roberta Persephone Moore.'

'How do you spell that?'

'Persephone?'

'Yes.'

'With difficulty.'

After taking down Mrs Moore's address, the policemen began their questioning.

'Can you explain why you've been acting suspiciously?' asked the Egyptian policeman.

'Acting suspiciously? In what way?'

'It has been noted that you have been walking around the hotel a lot.'

'Why shouldn't I walk around the hotel a lot? I'm paying good money to stay here!'

'While I appreciate that, Mrs Moore, it seems that some of the staff here find your behaviour unusual.'

'That's their problem rather than mine.'

'Can you explain why you've been walking around the hotel so much?'

'Is it essential that I explain myself?'

'If you can provide us with a proper explanation for why you have been walking around the hotel, we can be reassured that your behaviour isn't suspicious.'

'Fine,' she snapped. 'If you must know, it's because I've been very concerned about a friend of mine.'

'Is your friend staying at this hotel?'

'Yes, he is. However, I don't know which room he's in. In fact, I doubt he's in a room at all, he's far more likely to be in one of the suites. His name is Prince Manfred and I'm worrying about him because he's been unwell.'

'Prince Manfred of Bavaria?'

'The very same. I suspect he's in a suite on the third floor because I heard someone speaking German there. I shall keep to my room and the main communal areas from now on, if that's what you prefer.'

'I do not have a preference either way, Mrs Moore, it is up to you if you wish to continue walking around the hotel.'

'Well, it isn't, because the staff are clearly passing judgement on me for doing so and assuming that I'm wandering about murdering people.'

'No one is assuming that, Mrs Moore.'

'So why are you speaking to me about it then?'

'We merely wished to clear the matter up,' said the British policeman. 'And now that you've provided us with an explanation, we're happy that your behaviour is not suspicious.'

'How gracious of you to say so, officer.'

'I need to look at your passport.'

'Why?'

'We're looking at the passport of everyone we speak to.'

'Well it's in my room, I'll have to fetch it.'

'We can wait here while you do so, Mrs Moore.'

'Very well. I'm not sure how it's going to help with your investigation. What are you actually going to do about the death of the poor old lady?'

'We shall find the culprit.'

'How many guests are staying here?'

'Five hundred and twenty two.'

'Good luck with finding the culprit among that lot, then.'

AFTER HANDING the passport to the police officers, Mrs Moore, Lottie and Rosie went out onto the terrace. 'It's difficult to know what to do with oneself after a murder, isn't it Lottie?' Mrs Moore sank down into a wicker chair. 'I'd like to see some of the sights which Mr Villiers recommended, but it seems disrespectful to be enjoying myself.'

'I don't understand why Lady Harbottle is so upset about Mrs de Vere's death,' said Lottie.

'We all get upset when someone dies, don't we?'

'But I heard the pair of them arguing yesterday evening.'

'Really? What about?'

'Lady Harbottle was extremely upset that Mrs de Vere had been telling people about Lord Harbottle's children.'

'Not surprising I suppose, Mrs de Vere wasn't known for her tact was she?'

'But today Lady Harbottle said she was going to miss her enormously.'

'I suppose her upset with Mrs de Vere was forgotten about once she learned of the old lady's death. I expect Lady Harbottle calmed down after her outburst and is now just as devastated as everyone else by this senseless poisoning. Oh look, there's Prince Manfred's interpreter, do you recognise him Lottie?'

A slight man in a blue suit was climbing the steps of the hotel.

'I must speak with him!' Mrs Moore got up from her seat and dashed over to him. During the conversation, Lottie heard a loud motorcycle come to a halt out in the street.

Mrs Moore returned with a smile on her face. 'Apparently Prince Manfred is doing well and hopes to be up and about in a day or so! He had a fever which worried them for a bit, but now he's much improved. I'm so relieved! I was so worried he might die. I can't wait to see him.'

Mr Villiers appeared, carrying his motoring gloves and books.

'Are you talking about me, Mrs Moore?'

'No, Mr Villiers, why?'

'I heard you saying you couldn't wait to see someone and I assumed you meant me.' He flashed a grin.

'Oh? Well I... am always pleased to see you, Mr Villiers.'

'Are you? Oh good. And do call me Benjamin. How nice it is to see a friendly face. I'm going to sit here with you, if that's alright.' He placed his belongings on the table. Lottie hadn't noticed him reading any of his books yet.

'Was that you on that noisy machine just now, Mr Villiers?' said Mrs Moore.

'You mean my motorcycle? Yes it was me. I like to get out for a spin every day. Rain or shine. Actually, it's usually shine. It doesn't rain much here in Cairo.' He sighed and lit a cigarette. 'I don't know what to do with myself at a time like this,' he added.

'I feel exactly the same,' said Mrs Moore.

'Poor old Maggie, who could have done such a thing to her?'

'Hopefully the police will find the culprit soon enough.'

'They'd better do. It's not a nice thought knowing there's a poisoner in this hotel.'

'Why would someone poison Mrs de Vere?' asked Mrs Moore.

'I've no idea!'

'She seemed to have disagreements with people.'

'That's true, I'm just grateful I wasn't one of them.'

'You never disagreed with her?'

'Never.'

'Not even about the Pharaoh's Curse?'

'Oh, that was just a joke between us.'

He seemed dismissive of it now, but Lottie recalled he'd been so irritated by it the previous day that he'd left the conversation.

'I like a joke as much as the next man,' he continued, puffing out a cloud of smoke. 'In fact, I enjoy a joke *more* than the next man. We must remember, however, that when it comes to talk of the Pharaoh's Curse, that we are talking about the sad death of Lord Carnarvon and that should be treated with respect. Oh goodness, I've just had a thought.' His eyes fixed on a distant point.

'What is it, Mr Villiers?'

He turned to Mrs Moore. 'What if Margaret's death had something to do with the Pharaoh's Curse?'

'It couldn't possibly be. She never visited Tutankhamun's tomb, did she?'

'No, but she made light of the curse.'

'But the curse isn't real, is it?'

'I don't think so. Although I wear a cross to protect myself just in case, because you never know about these things.' He bit his lip anxiously.

'How can it be the Pharaoh's Curse if someone poisoned her?' asked Mrs Moore. 'Did the pharaoh tell them to do it?'

He gave a laugh. 'Now that you put it like that, Mrs Moore, you're right. I'm being foolish. I'm quite shaken up I suppose, I was there when it happened!' He ran a hand across his brow. 'Just awful. Poor old Maggie, she was a fascinating lady and I'm very sad she's no longer with us. I realise she wasn't everybody's cup of tea, but... oh dear, did I really say that? Excuse the slip. I realise she divided opinions, but she was the sort of lady you could fall out with one minute and then have breakfast with the next. She didn't bear grudges, and she didn't take things personally, she enjoyed sparring with people in her conversation. Many were offended by her words, but I wasn't bothered. She and I got on terrifically well.' He pulled out his handkerchief and wiped his eyes. 'I just can't believe she's gone. There has to be some sort of mistake, doesn't there? Perhaps that poison was intended for someone else. Perhaps it was intended for me? And it somehow ended up in the wrong cup.'

'Who could possibly wish to poison you, Benjamin? I can't imagine anybody wanting to do that.'

'There are a few archaeologists who are envious of some finds I've made on my digs. And then there's the lady back home who I once proposed marriage to.'

'And you didn't go through with it?'

'No.' He pulled a grimace. 'Rather naughty of me, I'm afraid. Once you think about it, you realise quite a lot of people probably wish to murder you, don't you?'

'Do you?'

'Oh yes, come now, Mrs Moore. Surely you've annoyed at least one person who might want you bumped off?'

'I sincerely hope not! What a terrifying thought!'

'Perhaps it's just me then. I apologise, Mrs Moore, I spoke out of turn. I like to have a bit of a joke and sometimes it gets out of hand. I'm sure nobody has any reason to murder you. I suppose what I'm trying to say is we're all flawed, aren't we? We all make mistakes and upset people, and then we've got to hope they don't turn out to be murdering maniacs. Otherwise we're in trouble then, aren't we?'

Chapter Nine

LOTTIE TOOK Rosie out for a stroll in the Ezbekiya Garden. The sun was strong, and she felt grateful for her broad-brimmed sun hat. Rosie walked slowly in the heat and Lottie didn't hurry her, instead she used the time to reflect on the strange events of the morning.

Who had poisoned Mrs de Vere?

Lady Harbottle was an obvious suspect because Lottie had heard how annoyed she was about Mrs de Vere's gossiping. But Benjamin Villiers was an obvious suspect too, surely he'd had the best opportunity to put poison in Mrs de Vere's tea? Lottie couldn't think what Mr Villiers' motive could be. He'd dismissed the talk of the Pharaoh's Curse as a joke and yet it had clearly bothered him at the time. Was it likely he'd poisoned her just because she'd teased him? Lottie decided not.

Perhaps the culprit was someone she'd never met before. The police had told them there were over five hundred guests in the hotel so the chance was high it could have been someone she hadn't come across yet.

There was also the possibility that Benjamin Villiers had

52

been the intended target. Although Lottie had solved similar puzzles before, this case seemed unusually difficult.

SHE ENCOUNTERED the young street hawker by the gnarled tree on her way back to the hotel. Rosie was keen to see him again, so Lottie allowed her to greet him. She admired the variety of colourful beaded necklaces he'd arranged neatly on a carpet over a trestle table.

'Bad news about Mrs de Vere, isn't it?' he said, patting the dog.

'Did you know her?'

'Not very well, but she lived at the hotel, so I knew who she was. She complained about my brother, Ahmed, once.'

'Why?'

'He once had to leave the kitchen to clear up a spillage in the restaurant and she complained he wasn't smartly dressed enough.'

'That wasn't very nice of her.'

'I heard she wasn't very nice. I have a friend who works on one of the cruise boats and she was rude to him once. And one of Ahmed's friends works as a waiter at Kursaal Music Hall. Apparently, Mrs de Vere said such bad things about the place that they lost customers.'

'Why did she do that?'

'She had a disagreement with the club owner, Miss Omar.'

Lottie recalled Mrs de Vere describing her club as disreputable and tawdry. 'What did they disagree about?' she asked.

'I don't know. But apparently Mrs de Vere had been telling the guests at Shepheard's Hotel that they shouldn't go there. That's why Miss Omar has been visiting Shepheard's a lot recently, she's been trying to find more customers. Ahmed's friend says Miss Omar has been worrying about money and how to pay her staff. Apparently they're all wondering if the club will close. Ahmed's friend doesn't want to lose his job there. I wonder if Miss Omar poisoned Mrs de Vere.'

'It sounds like she had a motive.' Lottie now recalled Lord Harbottle saying Mayar Omar had greeted Benjamin Villiers at breakfast. 'And she was there this morning!'

'Was she?'

'Yes. That's what I heard from one of the guests. She visited Mrs de Vere's table because she spoke to Mr Villiers.'

'I think I know who you mean, the archaeologist?'

'Yes.'

'So Miss Omar went to their table this morning... she could have put the poison in Mrs de Vere's tea because she was ruining her business.'

'I wonder if the police know about it?'

'We could tell them. Well you could, they wouldn't listen to me.'

'Why not?'

'Because they don't like people like me. They think I harass the tourists and try to cheat them out of their money. Now and again they decide I'm causing a nuisance outside this hotel and they move me on. Then I have to wait for a bit until I can come back and set up my stall again. They're nice to people like you, but for me it's a different matter.'

'That's unfair. We've spoken twice now and you've not tried to sell me anything.'

He smiled. 'I need to try harder, don't I? I'm not very good at selling necklaces.'

'They're pretty, I should buy one.'

'No, please don't.'

'Why not?'

'Because you'd only be doing it out of politeness.'

'Oh.'

'I should let you go on your way. It was nice to talk to you. My name is Karim, by the way.'

'I'm Lottie. And this is Rosie.' The dog gave a little bark, asking for another pat from Karim. 'Thank you for telling me about Miss Omar, it's interesting to learn some more about her.'

'She's an interesting person.'

'Could she actually have poisoned Mrs de Vere, do you think?'

'I don't know. It depends how desperate she was.'

Chapter Ten

'WHEN DID you last see Margaret de Vere?' asked Mr Mahmoud. He was a silver-haired, stern-faced official from the Ministry of Justice and spoke in French - the language preferred by Cairo's upper classes.

'This morning,' replied Mayar Omar. They sat in the hotel manager's office which Mr Mahmoud had commandeered for his interviews.

'When this morning?'

'At breakfast.'

'Did you speak to her?'

'I wished her a good morning, and I spoke briefly to the gentleman she was sitting with, Benjamin Villiers.'

'And what did you say to him?'

'I asked him if he would be visiting my club this evening.'

'And how did he reply?'

'He said that he would.'

'I've been told that you and Mrs de Vere were not on good terms.'

'No, we weren't.'

'Why not?'

'You know why not.'

His face stiffened. 'It's important that you explain it to me for the purposes of this interview.'

'She was always asking questions about the guests at my club. I thought we were friends and made the mistake of confiding in her once or twice. Then I realised she was using the information just to gossip, so I refused to tell her any more and she didn't take kindly to it. You know all this Hassan, we've chatted about it before, haven't we?'

A flicker of familiarity registered on his face, then he returned to his stern expression. Mayar tried not to laugh at the enforced formality.

'When did you last speak to her?'

'You've already asked me that.'

'Oh yes. What time did you arrive at the hotel this morning?'

'I stayed here overnight.'

'Overnight? Who with?'

'Must I tell you that?'

He gave an awkward cough. 'It would be useful.'

'For the investigation? Or for your own curiosity?'

'For the investigation, Miss Omar.' He coughed again, clearly uncomfortable.

'I spent the night alone, Hassan.'

'You must address me as Mr Mahmoud for the purposes of this interview.'

'What a shame.'

'Are you a regular visitor to this hotel?'

'You know I am.'

'And why did you spend the night here?'

'I have noisy neighbours and they keep me awake. The manager kindly allows me to stay here when I need to catch up on my sleep.'

His brow furrowed, as if he didn't quite believe her. 'How did you and Mrs de Vere become friends?'

'I like to be friendly with everyone. We got chatting on the terrace one afternoon and I consider everyone a friend until they do something unfriendly.'

'And what did she say this morning when you wished her a good morning?'

'She returned the greeting.'

'And was there any further conversation between you?'

'No, there wasn't. I then went over to a table at the far end of the restaurant. The first I knew something had happened to Mrs de Vere was when I saw a group of people gathered around her table. Then the waiters asked us to leave.'

'Did you approach her table?'

'No, I saw she was being attended to by a number of people, so there wasn't anything I could do. There were already enough people with her. Obviously, I was concerned about her, but I didn't think it was anything serious.'

'Where did you go after the waiters asked you to leave?'

'To the lounge.' She felt her heart thud a little faster as she told the lie.

'And how long did you stay there for?'

'I couldn't say to be certain, perhaps half an hour. During that time, I heard she'd died.' Mayar made her lower lip wobble, and a tear trickled down her cheek. She'd always been a good actress.

'Here, have my handkerchief.' He pulled it from his pocket and handed it to her.

'Thank you Hassan.'

'Not a problem.'

'I like the smell of this handkerchief. Which eau-de-cologne are you wearing?'

'Not now, Miss Omar.'

'You can call me Mayar, like you usually do.'

'Not in an interview.'

'You're always so professional, Hassan, that's what I like about you.' She wiped her eyes and gave him her best smile.

Chapter Eleven

In the hotel lobby, Lottie recognised the lady Mrs de Vere had dined with the previous evening. She had worn purple then but was head-to-toe in black today. She had grey bobbed hair and sat in a wicker chair with a fluffy white dog on her lap.

'Would you like to say hello to the other dog?' Lottie asked Rosie. She thought it could provide a good opportunity to speak to the lady about Mrs de Vere.

'Bonjour,' said the lady as Lottie and Rosie approached. Her dog bared its teeth. 'Maurice is not friendly, I'm afraid.' She spoke with a French accent. 'He thinks he should be the only dog in the world.'

Rosie sat and stared at him, and he uttered a little growl.

'We're sorry to bother you,' said Lottie, preparing to move away.

'You're not bothering me! Only Maurice, but we don't need to listen to him. What's your dog's name?'

They exchanged pleasantries about the dogs for a short while and the lady introduced herself as Madame Chapelle. Lottie then moved the conversation on. 'I noticed you dined with Mrs de Vere last night. I'm so sorry about the loss of your friend.'

'Oh, Margaret was a dear friend!' The lady's face crumpled, and she dabbed her eyes with a black handkerchief.

'Had you known her for long?'

'Not very long. Do sit down, child.' She pointed to a neighbouring chair and Lottie made herself comfortable while keeping Rosie a safe distance from snarling Maurice. 'I met Margaret here last year and then we corresponded with one another. I was so excited to be back in Cairo this year. I've had four lovely days here, and now this! I can't believe she's gone! Poisoned!'

'Did she mention if she'd upset someone?'

'Yes! Lots of people. Did you know Margaret?'

'A little.'

'She spoke her mind, didn't she? But she had so much character. My conversations with her were never boring, and she seemed to know absolutely everyone.' She wiped her eyes again. 'I fear that may have been her downfall.'

'What do you mean?'

'Presumably she knew something which someone wanted kept quiet.'

'Can you think of anything in particular?'

'Nothing at all! What would I know? I know Margaret socialised with many people here. Writers, explorers, actors, archaeologists, politicians, musicians, military men, just about anybody and everybody. She adored her life here, she was in the very centre of it all. But some people considered her a gossip and maybe she inadvertently shared something she shouldn't have. It wouldn't have been intentional, I know that. But she obviously offended someone. People worry too much about their reputation these days.'

'Did she tell you about her life before she came to Cairo?'

'Yes, a little. Her husband, Francis, was very wealthy and

they had a happy marriage, no children, but she was content with that. Children can be a lot of work and trouble, Lord Harbottle must know about that. Margaret's husband died twenty years ago, he drowned in a lake while saving a child.'

'The child survived?'

'Yes. Margaret told me that Francis sacrificed himself. He knew the dangers and yet he risked his life. It devastated her. I hope the child and its family were grateful.'

'They must have been.'

'You'd hope so, wouldn't you? What a good man Francis de Vere must have been. A man of his position could easily have ordered a manservant into the lake, but he went in himself. What an honourable gentleman. His family were landed gentry and, when he was a boy, a lucrative coal seam was discovered beneath their land. A great big colliery was built there and employed men from miles around. The pit machinery quite ruined the view from the house, apparently, but the family grew even wealthier.'

'Did Francis de Vere inherit the estate?'

'Yes, but Margaret sold it all after his death. She must have made a fortune from it.'

'Did she tell you much about her own family?'

'She was a Hawkins.'

'A what?'

'That was the family surname. Margaret's father was in the clergy, very senior. I think she told me he became a bishop.'

'Bishop Hawkins.'

'Yes, have you heard of him?'

'No. Did she have siblings?' Lottie wondered who would inherit Mrs de Vere's vast wealth.

'No, she was an only child. Her parents believed they could not have children, so Margaret's arrival was a pleasant surprise.'

'I wonder if Mrs de Vere's family in England has been informed of her death.'

'I wonder too! But I don't think she has much family, both her parents are deceased, and she had no siblings or children. I can only guess there's wider family somewhere, but she didn't tell me much about them. Sprigg is an unusual surname, where are your family from?'

'I don't know.'

'You don't know?'

'No, I'm an orphan.'

'Oh no, you poor little thing! Do you ever wonder who your parents were?'

'Sometimes. As a girl, I dreamt I was the secret child of a king and queen who would turn up one day and take me to live with them in their palace.'

Madame Chapelle smiled. 'What a wonderful dream! Perhaps it could still come true. Where did you grow up?'

'In an orphanage in Shropshire, England.'

'I've heard of Shropshire, even though I'm French. I think someone in Shropshire must know something about your family.'

'Perhaps they do, but I don't know how to find them.'

'With investigative skills! You need to find someone who's good at investigating things. Do you know anyone with those skills?'

Lottie smiled. 'Perhaps.'

Chapter Twelve

LOTTIE TOLD Mrs Moore about her conversation with Madame Chapelle as they readied themselves for dinner.

'She told me someone in Shropshire must know something about my family.'

'I think she's right. You were left as a baby on the doorstep of Oswestry Orphanage, your parents must have been local.'

'I wonder why they didn't come and find me.'

'Because it was probably complicated. If your mother had been a maid who'd got into trouble with the master of the house or his son, then it would have been difficult for her to admit to anyone she had a child. If that had been the case, I'm quite sure she would have wanted to see you but wouldn't have been able to. And perhaps she married and had more children and didn't feel able to tell anyone about her past. You know as well as I do, Lottie, how women are judged on their pasts.'

'I like the thought of having brothers and sisters.'

'You may well have some.'

'If only I could find them.'

'I'm afraid to say they're unlikely to know about you.'

Lottie felt saddened by this thought.

'Don't look so glum, Lottie. You have family here! Me and Rosie!'

Lottie smiled. 'You're both very good family to me.'

'And you are to me, too. My parents are both dead and I've had a succession of useless husbands. We all find ourselves alone in this world for different reasons, Lottie. But look what we have. We can still be happy!'

Lottie smiled. 'Yes, we can.'

'OVER HERE!' Lord Harbottle waved to Mrs Moore and Lottie as they arrived at the hotel restaurant for dinner that evening.

'I suppose we'd better be sociable, Lottie,' muttered Mrs Moore. 'Goodness, there's quite a crowd at the table this evening, isn't there?'

The Harbottles sat with Mayar Omar, Benjamin Villiers and Hugo Whitaker.

'Have you heard the latest, Mrs Moore?' said Mr Villiers, once they were sitting at the table.

'What's the latest?'

'Maggie's jewellery was stolen from her room.'

'No! When?'

'They think it happened shortly after she was poisoned.'

'Golly. All her jewellery?'

'I think so. Her maid reported it stolen.'

'Perhaps the maid took it,' said Lord Harbottle.

'Don't be so mean, Bartholomew!' said his wife.

'The maid must be extremely upset,' said Mr Whitaker. 'It's unkind to accuse her like that.'

'I speak only from experience,' said Lord Harbottle. 'Are you telling me you've never had a servant steal from you, Whitaker?'

'Never.'

'I think it's awful,' said Mrs Moore. 'Someone poisoned Mrs de Vere so they could go to her room and steal her jewellery?'

'It looks that way,' said Mr Villiers.

'I can't believe someone would be so heartless,' said Lady Harbottle. 'Poor Margaret.'

'Hopefully the police will catch them soon enough,' said Miss Omar. 'They'll probably try to sell the jewellery in a bazaar and they'll be discovered.'

'I hope so,' added Lord Harbottle.

'It just makes today's tragedy even worse,' said Miss Omar. 'I feel guilty I wasn't on good terms with Margaret when she died. It was a silly disagreement now that I look back on it. I shouldn't have let her bother me, but I did.'

'Don't be so critical of yourself, Miss Omar,' said Lord Harbottle.

'Oh, but I am! I feared she was asking me about my guests just so she could gossip about them, and then I avoided her! It was quite mean of me and I feel bad about it now.'

'She said some unpleasant things about your club,' said Mr Villiers.

Lottie recalled Karim telling her the same and how Miss Omar's income had been affected and that she'd been worrying about how to pay her staff.

'Yes, I heard she said some unpleasant things,' said Miss Omar. 'But there was no need for it to bother me.'

'She told some people to avoid your club altogether!'

'So I heard, Benjamin.'

'It must have affected your business.'

'No, it didn't affect business at all. I don't think many people paid much attention to what she said about the club.'

'Is your club busy?' asked Lord Harbottle.

'You've seen for yourself that—'

'No, I've never been to your club, Miss Omar.' He gave his wife a glance. She returned it with a sharp look, then glared at Miss Omar.

'No, of course. I was getting you confused with Benjamin here who has, of course, visited my club many times.'

'It's definitely been quieter recently,' said Mr Villiers.

'The numbers on the door don't suggest that,' said Miss Omar.

'Really? I got the impression it's not as busy as it used to be.'

'No. Still very busy, thank you, Benjamin.' Her lips thinned.

Miss Omar seemed keen to stress that Mrs de Vere's gossiping hadn't harmed her business at all. Lottie wondered if she was worried people could discover her motive for poisoning the old lady.

'If it helps you feel any better, Miss Omar, I must say that I feel awfully guilty too,' said Mr Villiers.

'Why, Benjamin?'

'I sat with Margaret at breakfast this morning and completely failed to notice who put poison in her tea!'

'You mustn't blame yourself,' said Lady Harbottle. 'The poisoner was clearly very clever.'

'But I do blame myself! How did I not spot them? She was murdered right in front of my eyes!'

'I'm sure if there was something you could have done, then you would have done it, Villiers,' said Lord Harbottle.

'I suppose so.' He sighed. 'I just wish I could have done more. Perhaps the Pharaoh's Curse visited Mrs de Vere after all.'

'Oh don't say such things!' said Lady Harbottle. 'We know the curse isn't real, anyway.'

'But it's spooky all the same,' said Lord Harbottle, shifting in his seat. 'Let's not talk of it again, otherwise we're all going to get horribly worried about our fate.'

The table fell into glum silence and the waiters arrived with bowls of onion soup. 'Shall we change the subject?' said Mr Whitaker.

'An excellent idea,' said Mr Villiers.

'I had to cancel the trip to the pyramids today,' said Mr Whitaker. 'But who'd like to join me tomorrow?'

'Me!' said Lady Harbottle.

'No, Polly,' said her husband. 'We're going to the races, remember?'

'We were supposed to have gone to the races today.'

'Yes, and we had to cancel because of the poisoning business. So we're doing the races tomorrow. And we've already done the pyramids, so I think we should do something else with our time.'

'Do you fancy the pyramids, Mrs Moore?' asked Mr Whitaker.

'Well, I suppose I could.'

'*Suppose*? You must! I can give you a generous discount.'

'Very well.'

'Excellent! You won't regret it. The cars leave from outside the hotel at ten o'clock tomorrow morning. We drive you to Giza and then we get on camels.'

'Oh golly!'

'It's enormous fun.' He gave a handsome grin, and Lottie noticed Lady Harbottle watching him with a smile.

'I've just remembered something,' said Lord Harbottle. 'I heard something at the Turf Club the other evening that I completely forgot to mention. I bumped into a chap there who once knew old de Vere.'

'Margaret's husband?' said Miss Omar.

'Yes. Francis I think his name was. This man I met had worked as a land agent in... oh wherever the de Veres had that coal mine. Derbyshire? Yorkshire? I can't remember. Anyway, the retired land agent had some dealings with the de Vere family and he knew Francis. Now I recall Margaret telling us a story about her husband having drowned while saving a child's life.'

'My goodness!' said Mrs Moore.

'My sentiments at the time,' said Lord Harbottle. 'Anyway, it turns out that it wasn't true. It was a complete cock and bull story. The land agent told me that old de Vere did nothing other than drink, chase after ladies and gamble. It all got the better of him and his heart gave up.'

'Oh dear,' said Lady Harbottle. 'So he didn't rescue a drowning child?'

'No.'

'So the poor child died?'

'No Polly, I don't think there was a child in the first place. It was all made up by Margaret to paint her husband in a good light.'

'But he was a drinker and a gambler?'

'Yes. And chased the ladies.'

'Did he ever catch one?' asked Mr Villiers with a chuckle.

'I couldn't say, old chap. But this land agent suspected that de Vere ran up enormous gambling debts. Rumour had it that Margaret had to sell the estate after his death to pay them all off.'

'So she wasn't rich?' asked Miss Omar.

'I suspect not.'

'But Mrs de Vere was clearly wealthy.'

'Was she?' replied Lord Harbottle. 'She might not have been.'

'How did she afford to live in this hotel all year round?' asked Lady Harbottle. 'It must cost a fortune. And she had all those fine clothes and jewellery.'

'She'd probably owned those for years, Polly. And as for

finding the board for this place, who knows how she managed that? Perhaps she negotiated a good discount.'

'So the fortune is all gone?' asked Mr Villiers.

'That's what the land agent chappy reckoned. It could just be rumour, but I'm tempted to think there's some truth in it.'

'Well I never,' said Miss Omar. 'Isn't it astonishing how some people present an image of wealth and success?'

'Quite astonishing,' said Mr Whitaker. 'It leaves you wondering if you can ever believe the things people tell you.'

Lottie couldn't agree more.

Chapter Thirteen

'ALL ABOARD FOR THE PYRAMID TOUR!' said Mr
Whitaker the following morning. He wore a white suit and
sun helmet and pointed Mrs Moore, Lottie and Rosie to a
shiny motor car.

'What a lovely day for it,' said Mrs Moore.

'It's always a lovely day for it here in Cairo.'

'How many of us are there on the tour this morning?'

'Twelve. The rest of the party should be here shortly,
meanwhile hop into the car and Sherif will drive you to the
dragoman and the camels. I'll meet you there.'

'Dragon man?'

'Dragoman.' He laughed. 'He's the guide.'

Their journey took them through the busy centre of
Cairo. The roof of the car was folded down and the warm
breeze brought odours of fresh bread, spices and animal dung.
The driver sounded his horn at donkeys, carts and cyclists and
exchanged loud insults with the driver of a tram. Rosie sat on
Lottie's lap, her tongue lolling as she took it all in.

There was a brief respite from the streets when they
crossed the bridge over the River Nile.

'There it is,' said Mrs Moore. 'The most famous river in the world! Apart from the Mississippi.'

'That's more famous?'

'Of course.'

'What about the Thames?'

'The Thames, Lottie? It's practically a trickle when compared to the Nile and the Mississippi.'

'A trickle?'

'I'm afraid so.'

Lottie gazed out over the glistening expanse of river and the boats with their tall white sails. She longed to cruise up the Nile to Luxor, then travel to the ancient Valley of the Kings. But was she brave enough to set foot in Tutankhamun's tomb? She couldn't be sure.

After travelling through a sprawling suburb of Giza, they arrived at a stretch of golden sand. The edge of the desert. Lottie's heart skipped as she saw the pyramids on the horizon.

'Look how close they are!' said Mrs Moore, admiring them through her lorgnette. 'Hopefully the journey on camelback will be quite short.'

Sherif, the driver, helped them out of the car and led them across the sand to where a group of camels knelt down, watched over by men in white robes. A man in baggy crimson trousers and matching cropped jacket greeted them. He had a thick black moustache and wore a white turban. Lottie guessed he was the dragoman.

'Greetings!' he said. 'What have you done with Mr Whitaker?'

'I believe he's on his way with the rest of the party.'

'Always late!' He laughed. 'Come and meet your camels.'

He led them to the nearest one which gave them a superior look as it ground its teeth. The large saddle on its back was covered in a rug with a colourful geometric pattern.

'Hello camel,' said Mrs Moore. 'I'm rather envious of your

lovely, thick eyelashes.' She turned to the dragoman. 'Does the camel have a name?'

'She's called Fahya.'

The camel twisted her lips, bared her teeth, then gave a long grunt.

'I don't think she likes me very much.'

'She is just being a normal camel.'

'How do I steer her?'

'You don't need to worry about that, Khaled the cameleer will guide her. And besides, she knows where she's going. She walks to and from the pyramids every day.'

'She won't run off?'

'Run? I've never seen this camel run. She's too lazy.'

'Is there a trick to getting on?'

'Yes, there is. You climb onto the saddle and arrange yourself so you're sitting side saddle with your feet draped to one side at the front. When you're comfortable—'

'Comfortable? I can't ever imagine being comfortable on a camel.'

'When you're as comfortable as possible, the camel will be instructed to stand. She will lift her hind legs first, so it's very important that you lean back to accommodate the movement of the camel. You can hold the handle at the front of the saddle. Then you can lean forward again as she raises herself up onto her front legs.'

'Golly, that sounds complicated. I'd rather ride a donkey. Have you got any donkeys?'

'Just camels, I'm afraid.'

'Very well then, camel it is.'

'It looks like the rest of the party is arriving,' said the dragoman, glancing at the road behind them. Lottie followed his gaze and saw two cars pulling up.

The dragoman turned back to Mrs Moore. 'Would you like to get on the camel now?'

'It's as good a time as any, I suppose.' She clambered up onto the saddle and arranged her legs to one side of it.

A group of well-dressed gentlemen got out of the vehicles. Meanwhile, Mrs Moore was looking uncertain on the saddle.

'Are you comfortable?' the dragoman asked her.

'No. I told you I wouldn't be.'

'Are you ready for the camel to stand up?'

'As ready as I'll ever be.'

The cameleer gave a command, and the animal lifted her hind legs.

'I lean forward?' said Mrs Moore.

'No, lean back!'

'Back?'

But she was leaning forward and, before the camel could raise her forelegs, Mrs Moore had somersaulted over the animal's shoulder and landed face first into the sand.

'Mrs Moore!' Lottie dashed over and pulled her employer's skirt and petticoat into a respectable position. 'Are you alright?' She took hold of an arm and helped her up. The dragoman picked up her sunhat and dusted the sand off it.

'Oh dear, oh dear,' said Mrs Moore. Her face was covered in sand and her eyes were screwed shut. 'I don't want to open my eyes Lottie, can you wipe my face with your handkerchief?' Lottie did so, careful not to rub at the sand too hard.

'Are you hurt?' asked the dragoman.

'No, only my pride is wounded. What happened?' She took the handkerchief from Lottie and continued wiping her face.

'You leaned forward instead of back,' said the dragoman. 'That's why you came off.'

'But that's what you told me to do!'

'I said lean back and then lean forward.'

'It's all so awfully confusing, no wonder I fell off. How embarrassing, I hope nobody noticed.'

'Only the rest of the party,' said the dragoman. The group of smartly dressed gentleman were now on the sand. One of them looked familiar. He wore a pale linen suit and was tall and plump. He had a curled moustache and wore a boater hat over his dark curls.

Mrs Moore wiped the last of the sand from her face and opened her eyes.

Then her sandy mouth fell open.

'Oh no!' she lamented. 'Tell me it's not true, Lottie! Did Prince Manfred of Bavaria just see my petticoat while I was face down in the sand?'

Chapter Fourteen

'ARE YOU ALRIGHT, MRS MOORE?' Mr Whitaker came dashing over. 'We all saw you fall.'

'You *all* did? Oh dear.'

'Are you hurt?'

'Not at all.' She rolled her shoulders back and took her sunhat from the dragoman. 'You know what they say when these things happen, you just have to get back in the saddle.'

'Absolutely, Mrs Moore!' said Mr Whitaker. 'That's the spirit!'

The prince's small, blue-suited interpreter approached. He wore an enormous sun helmet which gave him the appearance of a mushroom. Lottie stifled a giggle.

'Prince Manfred was most concerned to see you take a fall, he wishes to ask if you require any assistance at all?'

'No assistance needed at the present time,' said Mrs Moore. Her face reddened as she smiled at the prince and gave him a wave. 'But please thank him for his concern, I'm most grateful.'

The mushroom gave a polite bow and returned to the prince.

Lottie's camel was called Melwah, and she was a little smaller than Mrs Moore's camel. Once Lottie was in position, the cameleer handed Rosie to her so she could ride with her in her lap. Traipsing through the sand in the desert heat would have been quite a lot for the dog to contend with.

Eventually, everybody was seated on a camel and they set off across the sand. Once Lottie had grown accustomed to being so high off the ground, she began to enjoy the journey. The sun was high in the sky now and she felt grateful for her cotton long-sleeved dress and sun hat.

Before long, they reached the first pyramid.

'The Tomb of Khufu,' announced Mr Whitaker, steering his camel to the front of the group. 'Or the Great Pyramid of Giza. Our dragoman has some history for you.'

'It was built as a tomb for the pharaoh Khufu and was designed to be a monument to his power and glory,' said the dragoman. 'The pyramid was originally covered in smooth white limestone, which gave it a shining appearance in the sunlight. It was also once topped with a capstone made of solid gold.'

'How old is it?' asked Mrs Moore.

'Over four thousand years.'

'*What*?'

'It is built from over two million limestone blocks, each weighing over two tonnes. It is four hundred and eighty feet high.'

'Four thousand years ago?' said Mrs Moore. 'Before Jesus?'

'Two thousand years before Jesus,' said Mr Whitaker.

'No wonder they're called the Ancient Egyptians. They really were old, weren't they?'

'Very ancient indeed,' added Mr Whitaker.

Prince Manfred's interpreter spoke. 'The prince would like to know what's inside it.'

'A complex system of chambers and passages,' said the

dragoman. 'There's a burial chamber for the pharaoh and many smaller chambers and tunnels.'

'We can all dismount here and have a little walk around it,' said Mr Whitaker. 'Those brave enough to climb to the top can do so. You can even have a look inside it as well, if you like.'

'I'm quite alright where I am,' said Mrs Moore. 'I've successfully remained in the saddle so I'll stay here.'

LOTTIE DISMOUNTED and walked with Rosie up to the enormous pyramid. Some of the blocks were as tall as her. She placed her hand on the rough limestone, struggling to believe it had been carved so long ago.

Nearby, Prince Manfred and his chuckling companions helped each other up onto the blocks at the base of the pyramid. Mr Whitaker joined Lottie.

'Can you imagine what these structures would have looked like when they were encased in white limestone?' he said. 'They would have shimmered in the sunshine so brightly they must have blinded people. It's a shame the limestone casing was removed, it was used to help construct buildings and pathways in Cairo. Some of the medieval buildings in the city contain limestone from the pyramids. Look at the neighbouring pyramid there.' He pointed to it. 'That's the Pyramid of Khafre, you can see that its top retains some of the casing.'

'It's fascinating,' said Lottie. 'I can hardly believe I'm here!'

After looking around the pyramids, they moved on to the Sphinx.

'It has the head of a human and the body of a lion,' explained the dragoman. 'It's believed that the face is that of pharaoh Khafre. The statue was once painted in bright colours but everything has faded now.'

'I know that feeling,' said Mrs Moore. 'I'm fading fast on top of this camel. I need a lemonade in the shade.'

Her mood improved as Prince Manfred steered his camel towards her. And, as they made their way back across the sand to the cars, the interpreter joined them. Lottie listened to the conversation as she rode behind them.

'Prince Manfred is delighted to make your acquaintance again, Mrs Moore.'

'Please tell Prince Manfred that I'm delighted to hear it and I'm very flattered that he remembers my name.'

'Prince Manfred says he remembers you from Paris and Venice. He says you are almost as well travelled as him.'

'Please tell Prince Manfred that he is very observant indeed and that I enjoy travelling, it is one of my favourite hobbies. We clearly have something in common. Please will you ask Prince Manfred where he wishes to travel to next?'

'Prince Manfred never plans his journeys, he merely travels where the mood takes him.'

'Does he indeed? What a wonderful lifestyle to lead. Does he spend much time in his hilltop castle in Bavaria?'

'No he doesn't, he finds it cold and draughty.'

'That's a shame. Perhaps it needs modernising?'

'That would take a lot of work.'

'I think it probably just needs a woman's touch. You should see what my sister, Lady Buckley-Phipps did with Fortescue Manor in Shropshire. She turned a tumbledown stately pile into a comfortable home. The ladies in my family have a talent for such things. Perhaps you could mention that to the prince?'

Chapter Fifteen

BENJAMIN VILLIERS SAT opposite Mr Mahmoud from the Ministry of Justice and flashed him a grin. There was no response from the stern-faced investigator. Benjamin felt sure the grin would have lifted the mood if Mr Mahmoud had been female, the ladies usually liked his smile. But with Mr Mahmoud, he had no such luck.

'So you've brought me back in here again,' he said, glancing around the hotel manager's office. 'What have I done this time?'

'I warned you I would have to question you a few times,' said the investigator.

'To be fair, you did. Although there's nothing more I can tell you.'

'I need to check that your account of yesterday morning's incident is consistent.'

'You want me to tell you about it again?'

'Yes please.'

He didn't like the way Mr Mahmoud's dark eyes scrutinised his face. It made him feel twitchy and restless. And he didn't enjoy having to keep repeating himself, he knew it was a tactic to trip him up. 'So where do you want me to begin?' he asked.

'From the moment you entered the restaurant at breakfast yesterday morning.'

'Ah yes. So I went into breakfast and I saw—'

'What time was this?'

'Just after eight o'clock, like I told you before. I went in and saw Maggie - Mrs de Vere - sitting alone, so I thought I'd join her. I ordered bacon and eggs from the waiter and poured out a cup of tea from the pot on the table. Mind if I have a cigarette?' He needed something to calm his nerves.

'Go ahead. Did you pour Mrs de Vere some tea?'

'Yes. I asked her if she wanted a top-up and she said she did. Now I know that would have been the perfect opportunity to put poison in her tea, but I stress again that I didn't do such a thing. Nor did I notice anything in her cup which looked suspicious, merely the dregs of her previous cup of tea. So I sipped my tea and listened as Maggie told me about Lady Harbottle confronting her the previous evening about something she'd said about Lord Harbottle's children. Do you need me to tell you all about that again?'

'No, you may continue with your account.'

'Thank you.' He inhaled deeply on his cigarette. 'Anyway, speak of the devil and he shall appear, so the saying goes. Or *she* shall appear. Who turned up at that moment? Lady Harbottle. With her husband too. Mrs de Vere had to stop talking and I feel certain Lady Harbottle knew she'd been talking about her. So it was rather stiff and awkward when we exchanged our morning greetings and then the Harbottles went and sat somewhere else. Now I know what question you're going to ask next. Did I see Lord or Lady Harbottle put anything in Mrs de Vere's tea? No, I didn't. Could they have done so without me noticing? Possibly. I didn't exactly have my eye fixed on that cup of tea during our exchange, and why would I? I don't think either of them dropped anything into it, but I can't rule it out completely. Is it boring you having to listen to this again?'

'No, please continue.'

'Alright. So then we talked about a friend of Mrs de Vere's, a French lady I believe. Madame Chapelle or similar. Apparently, she had a terrible toothache and found a good dentist in the end and all was well. It wasn't a terribly interesting story, but I politely listened while I ate my bacon and eggs. Then Miss Omar stopped to say hello. It was only a quick greeting because she and Mrs de Vere didn't see eye-to-eye. But Miss Omar and I get on like a house on fire, so we had a brief conversation about me attending her club in the evening. That didn't happen in the end for obvious reasons, Miss Omar closed her club yesterday evening as a mark of respect. She's a good woman is Miss Omar. Did I see her put anything in Mrs de Vere's tea? No. Could she have done it without me noticing? Maybe. If I'd known that cup of tea was going to be poisoned, then obviously I'd have watched it like a hawk. But I didn't and there we have it. Then old Whitaker turned up.'

'Old Whitaker?'

'Hugo Whitaker. He wandered into breakfast just as I finished speaking to Miss Omar. He said hello, and I asked him to join us, he couldn't, however, because he wanted to have breakfast with the Harbottles. He's got a soft spot for Lady Harbottle, you see. And it's no secret that Lord Harbottle has, erm, interests elsewhere.'

'I don't think you told me this before. What interests?'

'Ladies. He likes to meet them at Miss Omar's club. Now Whitaker knows Harbottle does this, and he also knows that Lady Harbottle has a soft spot for him, too. So for that reason, he doesn't worry himself too much about being friendly with the chap's wife. Now I'm not saying it's the right thing to do, I consider it a little ungentlemanly myself. But Whitaker is quite taken with Polly Harbottle. Who wouldn't be? She's an attractive lady and quite wasted on old Harbottle. I wouldn't tell him that, of course, I consider both Harbottle and Whitaker to be good friends of mine. If I had to pick a side, then I'd go with Whitaker, but I've got nothing against Harbottle. If I were to offer Harbottle some advice, then I'd say he should leave the ladies alone and be faithful to his wife. And if he can't do that, then he should let her have a divorce and then she and Whitaker can get together. Isn't it astonishing how people complicate their lives? Anyway, I've strayed from the topic now. Where was I? Ah yes, Whitaker stopped to say hello, but I didn't see him put poison in Mrs de Vere's cup of tea. Does the fact I didn't see him put poison in her cup mean that he actually didn't? No. I can only tell you what I observed.'

'Did anyone else approach your table while you breakfasted with Mrs de Vere?'

'No, that was the lot.'

'And when was Mrs de Vere taken ill?'

'This is the distressing part.' He ran a palm down one side of his face. 'About two or three minutes after we spoke to Whitaker. She realised she hadn't drunk her tea, so she did so. Then she commented that something tasted odd, made a choking noise and... slumped to one side and slid off her chair. I was completely taken aback, in fact, I thought she was playing a joke on me to begin with. But when it had gone on too long, I leapt up and tried to help her as best as I could.' He felt a lump in his throat. 'The whole thing was just... terrible.'

'Indeed.' Mr Mahmoud shuffled some papers on the desk in front of him. Benjamin checked his watch, hoping he'd soon be dismissed. What else could the investigator possibly want to hear from him?

'Did you know Mrs de Vere kept expensive jewellery in her room?'

'I would have made the assumption she did because she was always wearing expensive jewellery. Now you're not accusing me of stealing it, are you? What would I want with it?'

'Did you go to her room after she was taken ill?'

'No!'

'Do you know of anyone else who went to her room after she was taken ill?'

'Absolutely not.'

'Very well.' Mr Mahmoud looked at his papers again. 'I've got your passport here,' he said. 'The photograph doesn't look like you.'

'Doesn't look like me?' Benjamin felt his heart thud. 'But of course it looks like me. It *is* me!'

Mr Mahmoud held up the passport and moved his eyes between it and Benjamin's face.

'You have more hair in the photograph.'

'I've had it cut since then.'

'Your hairline is a different shape.'

'It's changed a little over the years.'

'You look thinner.'

'Now or in the photograph?'

'In the photograph.'

'Darn it, I was hoping you'd say now. Well, I have gained a little weight over the years. A little less hair and a little more weight. Isn't that the way it goes?'

'And your nose is different.'

'I broke it a couple of months ago falling off a camel.'

Mr Mahmoud sighed. 'I realise you have an explanation for everything, Mr Villiers, but this photograph doesn't look like you.'

'It was taken a few years ago. Ten years even. And the

photograph was taken from an unusual angle, it's exaggerated some features and un-exaggerated others somehow. The overall result is a photograph which doesn't look a great deal like me. What more can I say?'

'Probably nothing, Mr Villiers.'

Chapter Sixteen

'POOR PRINCE MANFRED,' said Mrs Moore as she and Lottie sat on the terrace in the late afternoon sunshine. 'He told me he was so sick that he thought he would die! Can you imagine what that must have been like? Dreadful! He has suffered terribly. However, in celebration of his recovery he's hosting a show in the ballroom tonight and a special guest will be performing!'

'Who's the special guest?'

'I don't know, he wants it to be a surprise. The show is being put on for all the guests of the hotel. What a generous man he is Lottie. Always thinking of others.'

'You don't think the show is a little too soon after Mrs de Vere's death?'

'No, I don't think so, life has to go on, doesn't it? It's terribly sad that Mrs de Vere was poisoned, but everybody is doing everything they can about it and I don't see why five hundred hotel guests should have a thoroughly miserable time as a result. I hope I'm not speaking out of turn, Lottie, but it's quite clear that Mrs de Vere wasn't particularly well-liked, was she? Had she been more popular, then there would probably be a longer mourning period. But I think we've all spent some time feeling desperately sad about it all and we're now ready for some fun. Wouldn't you say?'

Lottie didn't want to disagree, so she gave a nod.

MRS MOORE WALTZED into the ballroom that evening in a voluminous pumpkin orange gown.

'You're a sight for sore eyes, Mrs Moore,' said Lord Harbottle, removing a large cigar from his mouth. 'Couldn't you have chosen something a little more colourful?'

'This isn't colourful enough?'

'I was having a joke. You look wonderful, I've little doubt the prince will notice you this evening.'

'Thank you, Lord Harbottle.' She took a seat next to Mr Villiers and Lottie sat next to Lord Harbottle. Lady Harbottle sat on the other side of her husband and wore a lilac dress of layered organza and a sparkling headband in her blonde hair. Mr Whitaker sat next to her and looked handsome in his dark dinner suit.

'I hope you've fully recovered now, Mrs Moore,' said Mr Whitaker.

'Oh yes, absolutely.'

'Recovered from what?' asked Lady Harbottle.

'I took a little tumble off a camel,' said Mrs Moore.

'How awful!'

'I was fine, I didn't fall far, and it was a soft landing in the sand.'

'Camels are strange things,' said Lady Harbottle. 'I much prefer motor cars.'

'But the motor car can't get across the sand, can it, Polly?' said her husband. 'We like to think we're terribly clever by inventing the combustion engine but, sometimes, the old methods of transport are the most reliable.'

'But only in the desert,' said his wife. 'We have little call for camels at home, do we, Bartholomew?'

'There's not a great deal of sand in London, that's for sure.'

'Or anywhere other than the beach.'

'Do you like the beach, Polly?' asked Mr Whitaker.

'I love the beach!'

'So do I.'

'The last time we went to a beach, Polly, you complained that the sand got in your hair and the sea was too cold for bathing,' said Lord Harbottle. He took a puff on his fat cigar.

'That's because it was a beach in Britain. If it had been a beach in the Caribbean, then I would have been much happier.'

'Have you been to the Caribbean, Polly?' asked Mr Whitaker.

'Yes, I adore it there!'

'So do I.'

'Where's the prince?' asked Mrs Moore, surveying the ballroom through her lorgnette. Each table was filled with guests and red velvet curtains were pulled across a stage at the far end of the room.

'I'm sure he'll turn up in a moment,' said Mr Villiers. 'I'm looking forward to seeing the man they call Europe's most eligible bachelor.'

'I'm very excited to see what entertainment he's got lined up for us,' said Mrs Moore. 'Wouldn't it be amusing if he did a turn himself?'

'Perhaps he sings?' said Lord Harbottle.

'Or maybe he's got some funny jokes?' said Mr Villiers. 'I hope this evening doesn't drag on too long, I fancy a turn at the Turf Club later. Do you fancy it too, Harbottle?'

'I'd say that I do, Villiers.'

Lottie noticed the two men exchange a wink.

The room hushed as the hotel manager climbed onto the stage. 'Ladies and gentlemen, I am humbled by the enormous honour I have this evening of introducing to you a fine gentleman of great worthiness and distinction. His Royal Highness Manfred Ludwig Franz Wilhelm Prinz von Bayern!'

The room erupted into applause.

The prince strode onto the stage in a pistachio green jacket and royal purple trousers. A purple silk cravat was tied at his neck and his dark brown curls were luxuriantly glossy. The blue-suited interpreter joined him on the stage.

Prince Manfred spoke in German, and his companion translated the speech for everybody. 'My esteemed ladies and gentlemen and guests of the venerated Shepheard's Hotel. It is a great honour to be staying with you here in this magical oasis in the ancient city of Cairo. I expect many of you have explored the city and its environs, personally I am looking forward to visiting the magnificent sites of this ancient land. I have suffered some ill health since my arrival and have been delayed in my appreciation of all the wonders Egypt has to offer. In celebration of my recovery, I have organised a show and hopefully it will cheer us up after the recent tragedy. I was most saddened to hear about the death of Mrs de Vere. Although I didn't know her personally, I have been hearing wonderful things about her and she will be sorely missed by everyone. I am also certain she wouldn't have wanted her fellow guests to be spending the rest of their stay in Cairo in misery. She would have given us her blessing for the show to proceed.'

More applause broke out. 'Hear, hear!' shouted Lord Harbottle.

'I present to you now a beautiful woman who I've had the great pleasure of becoming acquainted with since my arrival here in Cairo.' Lottie noticed Mrs Moore's expression turn stony. 'So, without further ado, I invite onto the stage for you now the extremely talented performer, Miss Mayar Omar!'

Everyone clapped apart from Mrs Moore.

A veiled and barefoot Miss Omar stepped onto the stage. She was swathed in sheer fabrics and embellished with sequins and beads which sparkled under the lights. She struck a pose, gave a brief nod to someone at the side of the room, and then began to dance as the shrill of a woodwind pipe rose and fell over the heavy thud of drums. The music sounded a little discordant to Lottie, but it was also mysterious and haunting. Miss Omar's limbs waved and whirled, and the beads on her costume jangled.

Lottie glanced at the faces around her table. The men were enthralled and Lady Harbottle seemed pleasantly entertained. Mrs Moore, however, sat with her arms folded and her mouth in a sulky pout.

More songs followed. Some dancers joined Miss Omar, then she sang a few tunes in a language Lottie couldn't understand. She guessed it was Arabic. Or was it Persian?

When the show was over, the applause was rapturous and Prince Manfred appeared on stage with an enormous bouquet. He kissed Miss Omar on each cheek as he presented her with the flowers, then held her hand as they both bowed.

Mrs Moore was the first to leave.

'WHAT A WASTE OF AN EVENING,' said Mrs Moore once she and Lottie were in her room. Rosie had been dozing on her bed and observed them through sleepy, blinking eyes. 'We should have had a game of cards on the terrace instead. I had no idea Miss Omar was acquainted with the prince, did you?'

'I had no idea at all.'

'Why? And where and how did she even meet him?'

'She'll probably tell you if you ask her.'

'I don't want to ask her. It will make me seem like I'm interested and I'm not. Perhaps you could ask her?'

'I can if you'd like me to,' said Lottie. 'Miss Omar is the sort of lady who knows a lot of people. She makes it her job because she owns a nightclub and wants to make sure as many people as possible go to it.'

'You don't honestly think that Prince Manfred would go to her awful nightclub do you?'

'I don't know. She must have invited him. It seems to be the sort of place that gentlemen like to go to.'

'But not Prince Manfred, I can't imagine it's his sort of place at all. I'm quite surprised he has anything to do with her.'

'Miss Omar has been perfectly nice whenever I've spoken to her.'

'I'm sure she has been Lottie, but everyone says she has loose morals. I really thought Prince Manfred was better than that.' She slumped into a chair by the window with a sigh. 'I don't understand what he sees in her. In fact I *do* understand what he sees in her, it's what all the gentlemen see in a lady of beauty and grace. But for some reason I thought Prince Manfred was different.' She gave another sigh. 'You think you know someone and then it's completely heart-breaking when you realise you don't know them at all.'

Chapter Seventeen

LADY HARBOTTLE KEPT herself awake that evening by reading one of her favourite romance novels. She wanted to stay awake until her husband returned from his supposed visit to the Turf Club. She didn't doubt that he went to the Turf Club, but she suspected he also frequented Miss Omar's club. She was looking forward to questioning him about it when he returned. She knew he was hopeless at lying after a few whiskies.

She was enjoying the novel, the hero reminded her of Hugo Whitaker. They had enjoyed a drink together after Bartholomew and Benjamin had left. Hugo had implored her to stay for another, but she'd reluctantly retired for the night because she didn't want people to talk. It was tempting, however, to throw all caution to the wind and embark on a love affair with Hugo. Would it be so terrible?

It had been a mistake to marry Lord Harbottle, she realised that now. She hadn't married for love, she'd married for status and now that decision had come back to haunt her. Why had she always been attracted to important men? She regretted her affair with Sir George Efford because of the publicity and embarrassment it had caused them both. She hadn't loved him either, and yet the affair had ended his marriage. What a lot of upset for nothing! She had found it difficult to get acting roles after the scandal too, her name had been too much of a distraction for theatre audiences. She'd been lucky to get the role in *Lady Windermere's Fan* but it was that play which had led to Lord Harbottle spotting her. If only she had turned him down.

As for Hugo, he was just a normal kind gentleman who'd fought in the war then stayed in Egypt afterwards. She finally knew what it was like to feel genuine affection for someone. And he was so handsome too! She wished she'd met him sooner, before she came across Efford and Harbottle. Life could be cruel like that. Although her husband's infidelities angered her, she only hoped he'd run off with another woman and divorce her. Then she would be free!

But perhaps she wouldn't need to wait for that, maybe there was a simpler option. A little bit of poison in his tea, perhaps? She pushed the thought away, it was too tempting. She returned to her book.

She read a few more chapters before the bedroom door opened and Bartholomew staggered in, red-faced and grinning. He walked as if he'd forgotten how to bend his knees.

'Hello darling, you're still awake?' he slurred.

'Yes. Can you close the door, please?'

'Oh yes! Whoopsy.' He went back to the door and closed it with too much force.

'Not so noisy, Bartholomew! You must have drunk a lot.'

'I'm sorry, I what?' He weaved his way towards the bed.

'I said you must have drunk a lot.'

'Yes, I mean *no*. I didn't have that much.' He stank of cigarettes and whisky. 'How's my lovely wife?'

'A little tired. Did you have a nice evening?'

'Yes, a lovely time.'

He took off his jacket and dropped it onto the floor. Then he thought better of it and picked it up again and attempted to brush it down with his hand.

'Who was at the club this evening?'

'Who was at the club this evening?' He was repeating her question to give himself time to think. 'Well, obviously Villiers was there.' He put his jacket on the back of a chair and it slid off.

'Yes, I know that because you went with him.'

'And who else was there? Just let me think.... tum-te-tum... a chap called Carruthers, British Army. Another army chap, Blenkinsop. And there was a retired Eton schoolmaster whose name I've forgotten... Smith, I think it was. Anyway, thoroughly enjoyable company. What happened to that... what's his name again? That man. Whitaker! Where's he gone?'

'To his room, I imagine.'

'Insolent man. He likes you, I can tell.'

'Most people like me, I think.'

'No, but I mean he likes you as in *likes* you.' He slumped into a chair, his chin resting on his chest.

'I'm surprised you didn't go to Miss Omar's club. What's it called again?'

'Kursaal something-or-other. Kursaal Music Hall. Why would I go there?'

'After Miss Omar's performance this evening, I thought you might like to see more of the dancing girls.'

'Dancing girls? No, not the dancing girls. I don't like dancing girls. I only have eyes for my wife.' He grinned.

'I don't think that's quite true, is it?'

'What do you mean, it's not true? Of course it's true.'

'I think you go to Miss Omar's club to see the dancing girls just like you go to those clubs in Soho at home.'

'Oh, that was only a few times.'

'I think it was lots of times, wasn't it Bartholomew?'

'Lots of times? No. I didn't go again after you told me off about it.'

'I think you did.'

'Why are you arguing with me? I've had a lovely evening and now you're arguing with me.'

Lady Harbottle felt her teeth clench in anger. She closed her book and placed it on her nightstand.

'Are you going to sleep now?' asked her husband. He'd slipped down in his chair and his eyelids were heavy.

'Yes, I'm going to sleep. I'm pleased you had a nice time at the Kursaal Music Hall.'

'I had a lovely time.' His eyes were practically closed now. She felt no inclination to help him into bed. If he was comfortable in the chair then she would leave him to sleep there.

'Goodnight, Bartholomew,' she said, turning off the light.

There was no response, but moments later, a loud snore came from the direction of the chair.

Lady Harbottle covered her ears with pillows. How she wished Hugo was with her now instead.

Chapter Eighteen

'OH, MY HEAD!' said Mrs Moore. She lay in bed, her sleep mask still over her eyes.

'Are you sure you won't have any breakfast?' Lottie asked her.

'Absolutely sure. I can't face it. I couldn't even walk at the moment, let alone face any food. The headache powders aren't working and I feel as though I shall be lying here forever!'

Although her employer was prone to melodrama, Lottie still felt sorry for her. The friendliness between Prince Manfred and Miss Omar the previous evening had dismayed her. Lottie felt sure there was no genuine affection between the pair and that their familiarity had been part of the show, but Mrs Moore feared the worst.

'Rosie and I shall go down to breakfast if that's alright,' she said.

'Yes, please do! I'm no use here to man nor beast. I'm afraid you'll have to entertain yourself today, Lottie.'

. . .

AFTER BREAKFAST, Lottie took Rosie for a walk in Ezbekiya Garden, then stopped to talk to Karim the street hawker on her way back to the hotel. Rosie was very happy to see him, her tail didn't stop wagging.

'They've not caught the poisoner yet?' he said.

'Not yet.'

'It's not going to be easy.'

'No, it's not. Do you remember telling me about your brother's friend who works as a waiter at Miss Omar's nightclub?'

'Yes.'

'And he said the club was in financial trouble and that he was worried about losing his job?'

'Yes, because Mrs de Vere had told people not to go there.'

'Could that really be true?'

'Why wouldn't it be?'

'Well, at dinner the other evening, Mr Villiers mentioned to Miss Omar that Mrs de Vere had told people to stay away from her club. He said he'd noticed the club was quieter than it used to be and she denied it.'

'That's strange,' said Karim. 'Because if you speak to the people who work there, they'll tell you she's quite worried about it.'

'So that suggests Miss Omar lied the other evening. Maybe she wants to pretend everything is going well at the club because she doesn't want anyone to suspect she could have poisoned Mrs de Vere in revenge for ruining her business.'

Karim's eyes widened. 'You've caught her out!'

'I don't know if I have or not. But she has a motive for murdering Mrs de Vere, doesn't she?'

'You should tell the police.'

'I only want to do that if I'm sure about something, I'm not sure about it yet. I don't want to get into trouble.'

'With who?'

'People who don't want to be investigated by the police. They can turn nasty.'

'That's happened to you before?'

'Yes, and I don't want to make that mistake again.'

'Perhaps you need to forget about the poisoning for now and leave the investigator to do his work. What are you planning to do today?'

'I don't know yet, my employer is unwell and resting.'

'Oh no, is it serious?'

'I don't think so, hopefully she'll recover soon.'

'Perhaps you would like to see some sights of Cairo?'

'I would, but wouldn't know where to start.'

'I can show you.'

'You're busy, you've got your jewellery to sell.'

'It's boring, and I sold quite a lot yesterday. I'd like to do something different for a day.'

Lottie liked this idea. 'If you have time, then I'd love to see a few sights! How much do I need to pay you?'

Karim laughed. 'No payment needed! Just some money for the tram. I need to pack away my stall. Shall I meet you here again in fifteen minutes?'

'That sounds perfect.'

FIFTEEN MINUTES LATER, they set off to catch a tram. Further down the street, they passed a sprawling hotel which looked even larger than Shepheard's, with rows of windows and balconies.

'The Grand Continental,' said Karim. 'That's where Lord Carnarvon died a few weeks ago.'

Lottie gave a shudder. 'Do you believe in the Pharaoh's Curse?'

'No. But it's a good story, isn't it? Let's run for the tram!'

. . .

A SHORT WHILE LATER, they stepped from the tram onto a hot, dusty street lined with palm trees. Ahead of them rose imposing fortress walls on a hill. Beyond the walls were gleaming white domes of a mosque with pointed minarets stretching tall into the blue sky.

'The citadel,' said Karim. 'A fortress built by my ancestors to protect themselves against your ancestors.'

'Really?'

'It was built by the ruler Saladin during the crusades eight hundred years ago. There are lots of buildings within the walls, palaces and military barracks. But that building you can see is the Great Mosque of Muhammad Ali Pasha.'

'It's very impressive,' said Lottie. 'Mrs Moore would like to come and see this.'

'I can show her when she's feeling better.'

They walked around the citadel walls.

'How long have you worked for Mrs Moore?' asked Karim.

'Just a few months. Before then I worked as a maid in her sister's house.'

'In England?'

'Yes, in a large country house surrounded by rolling green hills. Completely different to here!'

'I should like to visit one day.'

'You must.'

'When I've saved up lots and lots of money for the journey, I'll write you a letter to let you know I'm on my way. I need to warn you that I'll be an old man by then.'

Lottie laughed. 'You never know what life may bring, Karim. I grew up in an orphanage and never imagined I'd travel like I am now. It was a surprise turn of events, I've been very lucky.'

'It's not luck.' He smiled. 'It's because you're a nice person.'

Lottie felt her face heat up. She didn't know what to say.

'Do you know how I know when someone is a nice person?' he continued. 'When they have a nice dog.'

They both looked down at Rosie who returned their gaze with her large, dark eyes.

'Have you visited the Egyptian Museum yet?' asked Karim.

'Not yet.'

'What have you been doing with your time?' He laughed.

'I saw the pyramids yesterday, does that count?'

'Yes, that counts for something.'

THEY TOOK another tram to the museum. The journey gave Lottie time to think as the tram bumped its way through Cairo's chaotic streets. She cuddled Rosie on her lap and thought about the conversations of the past few days. Miss Omar wasn't the only person whose words and actions seemed inconsistent.

'I think Lady Harbottle is suspicious,' she said to Karim. They could just hear each other over the noise of the tram. 'I overheard her confronting Mrs de Vere about her gossip and she seemed furious at the time. But after Mrs de Vere was poisoned, Lady Harbottle was extremely upset and described her as a nice, welcoming person.'

'People say things like that about someone after they've died.'

'They do. But she didn't need to say it, did she? She could have just said something respectful about her and left it at that. But instead she was crying and talking about how sad she was. It seemed as though she was putting on a show.' Lottie hadn't forgotten that Lady Harbottle had once been an actress.

'You think she was trying to prove how upset she was?'

'Yes, I think she was.'

'Which is what someone might do if they don't want to be suspected of murder. So you suspect two people now, Miss Omar and Lady Harbottle?'

'Yes, and someone else too.'

'Tell me in a moment, we're coming up to our stop.'

THE EGYPTIAN MUSEUM was built in a striking pink stone and had tall arched windows. Inside, the cool marble interior provided welcome relief from the heat. Ancient statues and sarcophagi were displayed on rows of stone plinths.

'This is fascinating!' said Lottie, moving from one exhibit to the next. 'How wonderful to see things like this up close!'

'You were going to tell me about the other person you suspect,' said Karim.

'Oh yes. Benjamin Villiers.'

'The man who was having breakfast with Mrs de Vere?'

'Yes. The previous day, he had walked away from a conversation with her because she'd been teasing him about the Pharaoh's Curse. So why did he choose to have breakfast with her the following morning? He said the Pharaoh's Curse had been a joke between them, but he seemed genuinely annoyed when he left the conversation.'

'So you think he's someone else who is pretending she didn't bother him as much as she did?'

'Exactly.'

'Suspicious.'

IT WAS late afternoon when they emerged from the museum, blinking in the bright sunlight.

'Have you got time to look at the river?' said Karim. 'It's close by.'

'Alright, and after that I must get back. Mrs Moore will be wondering where I've got to. I've had a lovely day though, thank you for showing me around.'

He smiled. 'It's been a pleasure.'

From the museum, they followed a path to the riverside. They passed a terminus for one of the tram lines and reached a stone embankment from where they could look out at the river.

'That's Gezira Island,' said Karim, pointing to the opposite bank. 'It sits in the middle of the river. It has some botanical gardens and a sporting club. If you have time while you're staying here, you should visit the gardens.'

Behind them, a tram rumbled into the stop.

'I'm sure Mrs Moore will enjoy the gardens too,' said Lottie. 'I'll suggest it to her this evening.'

A movement caught the corner of her eye. She turned to see a tall man walking along the riverbank with a brown leather case in one hand. He seemed familiar.

'What is it?' said Karim.

'I've just realised who that is,' she whispered. 'It's Lord Harbottle!'

'Really? What's he doing here? He must have just got off the tram.'

'And what's he doing with that case in his hand?'

'Let's see where he goes.'

'I don't want him to notice us.'

'We can keep our distance.'

They followed him for a short while, then stopped beneath the shade of some trees. Lord Harbottle also stopped and looked around him as if checking to see who was about. Lottie picked up Rosie and retreated into the shadows. 'He's up to something,' she whispered.

'Maybe he's here to meet someone and is going to give them the case,' said Karim. 'Maybe it's got money in it?'

Lottie looked around, there was no one else about.

Lord Harbottle checked around him again before lifting his arm and hurling the case into the water. It landed with a splash. Then he lit a large cigar, turned on his heel and marched back the way he'd come. Lottie, Karim and Rosie ducked behind the trees and watched him pass. To Lottie's relief, he didn't glance in their direction.

'What did he do that for?' said Karim, once Lord Harbottle was out of sight.

'I've no idea,' said Lottie. 'Do you think he's gone?'

'He must have gone back to the tram.'

Cautiously, they crept out of their hiding place and made their way to the spot where Lord Harbottle had thrown the case into the water. There was no sign of it.

'How annoying,' said Lottie. 'I thought we could fish it out again.'

'Fish it out?' Karim laughed. 'No chance of that.'

'It's such a shame we can't retrieve it!' said Lottie. 'I wonder what's in it? Obviously something he doesn't want anyone else to find. Where does the river go from here?'

'It flows north to the Nile Delta and then to the sea about a hundred miles away.'

'So the suitcase could end up in the sea?'

'Yes, unless someone finds it first. It could wash up on a bank.'

'Lord Harbottle must be destroying evidence,' said Lottie. 'And it has to be connected to Mrs de Vere's murder.'

Chapter Nineteen

LOTTIE HEARD MRS MOORE'S laughter as she climbed the steps of Shepheard's Hotel. When she reached the terrace, she saw her employer looking remarkably different to the woman she had left that morning. She wore a pastel blue dress and was sharing a joke with Lady Harbottle, Mr Villiers and Mr Whitaker.

'Lottie!' She peeked at her through her lorgnette then waved her over to the table. 'Where have you been?'

'To the citadel and the Egyptian Museum.' She decided not to mention the river in case Lord Harbottle heard she'd been there.

'Golly, how did you get to those places?'

'By tram. Karim accompanied me.'

'Karim?'

'The young man who sells necklaces.'

'That street hawker?'

'Yes, it was very kind of him to show me around.'

'Splendid chap!' chuckled Mr Villiers. 'He knows a pretty face when he sees one!'

'He didn't try to sell you a necklace?' asked Mrs Moore.

'No. Are you feeling recovered now?'

'Very much so. And, in fact, I have some wonderful news. Come and join us, Lottie.'

She did so, seating herself between her employer and Lady Harbottle.

'You'll never guess who spoke to me about an hour ago,' said Mrs Moore with a wide smile.

'Who?'

'Prince Manfred's interpreter. He came up to me, right here!'

'He did,' said Mr Whitaker. 'I saw him.'

'And do you know what he said? He told me that the prince would like to invite me to dinner.'

'Really?'

'Yes! Isn't it wonderful? On Friday evening.'

'In three days' time.'

'Yes. Three days to wait. I don't think I can bear to wait that long, Lottie! But he's a very busy man so I must be patient.'

'That's lovely news. It is just you who he's invited is it? There won't be three hundred other people like there were for the invitation in Paris?'

'No, I checked that with him and it will just be the two of us! Well, three of us when you include the interpreter. In fact, I must get reading *Colloquial German* again, I have three days in which to learn some more German. I think I should be able to learn quite a bit.'

'You've clearly caught the man's eye,' said Mr Whitaker.

'Thank you, Hugo.' She gave a coy smile. 'I suppose it's what I set out to do.'

'And you've done very well,' said Lady Harbottle. 'He seems a charming man.'

'Oh, he is.'

'Let's raise a toast!' said Mr Villiers. 'To Mrs Moore and her Prince Charming!'

Mrs Moore giggled, and everyone raised their glasses. Lottie didn't have one, but she was pleased to see her employer happy again.

'Thank you everybody,' said Mrs Moore. 'I'll make sure I invite you all to my hilltop Bavarian castle!'

'What's the cause for celebration?' came a voice from close by. Lottie turned to see Lord Harbottle approaching.

'Oh there you are, Bartholomew, I was wondering where you'd got to,' said Lady Harbottle.

'I went for a stroll in the gardens and dozed off on a bench! Can you believe it?'

No, Lottie wanted to reply, but she bit her lip and kept quiet.

'Sleeping off the drink from last night, Harbottle?' said Mr Villiers with a laugh.

'I didn't have that much to drink, old boy.' He gave his wife a wary glance.

'Ah no, of course not. Well pull up a chair and join us, we're celebrating Mrs Moore's invitation for dinner with Prince Manfred of Bavaria.'

'Dinner with the prince, eh? That sounds very impressive, indeed. Do you have designs on the gentleman, Mrs Moore?'

'What a direct question, Lord Harbottle!' She giggled again and smoothed her dress. 'I suppose it's no great secret that I'm on the lookout for a husband, but I won't be suggesting such a thing to the prince at dinner, I don't want to scare him off!'

'No, you don't want to do that,' said Mr Whitaker. 'But you'll need to make your intentions known sooner rather than later, us chaps don't always read the signs, you know. In fact, the mysteries of a lady's mind can be quite a puzzle to us sometimes.' His eyes were on Lady Harbottle as he spoke. 'Sometimes a chap just needs to know where he stands.'

'May I request that you don't gaze at my wife in that manner, Whitaker?' said Lord Harbottle.

'I'm sorry?'

'I don't like the way you're looking at my wife.'

'And I don't like the way you're speaking to me, Harbottle.'

'You should expect it after the manner in which you've been making eyes at her over the past few days. I've let it pass several times, but now, quite frankly, I've had enough!'

'Would this be the same wife you abandoned yesterday evening, Harbottle?'

'*Abandon*? I didn't abandon her. I merely went to the Turf Club, a reputable gentleman's club around the corner. I would have taken my wife with me but women aren't allowed in there. I've little doubt that you made the most of the opportunity and spent the evening in her company, am I right?'

'She would have otherwise spent the evening alone.'

Lord Harbottle gave a snort. 'Alone? Among all these other guests she's made friends with? You paint yourself as a knight in shining armour merely as an excuse to move in on another man's wife. Well it won't do, I tell you. It won't do!'

To Lottie's dismay, Lord Harbottle got to his feet. Mr Whitaker did the same.

Mr Villiers also stood up. 'Gentlemen, please. There's no need for this. I'm sure we can settle this misunderstanding with a calm discussion.'

'The only thing which will settle matters is that man staying away from my wife!' said Lord Harbottle.

Lady Harbottle burst into tears and left the table.

'Now look what you've done, Harbottle!' said Mr

Whitaker. 'Do you think upsetting your wife and causing a scene is going to solve anything?'

'Stay away from us!' Lord Harbottle pointed a finger in his face. 'Before I do something I might regret!' He stormed off after his wife.

Chapter Twenty

Mrs Moore and Lottie dined quietly in the hotel restaurant that evening. There was no sign of the Harbottles. Benjamin Villiers and Hugo Whitaker arrived late and sat at a table together on the far side of the restaurant.

'I thought Lord Harbottle and Mr Whitaker were going to come to blows earlier,' said Mrs Moore. 'What a way to behave! I hadn't noticed Hugo making eyes at Lady Harbottle, had you?'

'I'm afraid I did.'

'Golly! And you didn't tell me?'

'I didn't want to gossip.'

'That's a fair point, we all saw what happened to the hotel gossip, didn't we? What a tragedy. Anyway, I shall cheer myself up with thoughts of Friday evening with Prince Manfred. I never thought he would ask me! After yesterday evening, I thought he was going to run off with Miss Omar.'

'It was just a performance, there was nothing between them.'

'I realise that now! Oh, how silly I was. And yet now I can

think of nothing but Friday evening. It's the reason we came here to Cairo!'

A KNOCK at Lottie's door woke her early the following morning. A maid had a message for her. 'Karim would like to speak with you,' she said. 'He's waiting at the reception desk.'

'Do you know what he wants?'

She shook her head.

'What's the time?'

'Seven o'clock.'

Lottie splashed some water over her face at her washstand, then hurriedly dressed. What could Karim possibly want at this hour?

She hurried down the stairs with Rosie and saw him waiting in the lobby. He grinned as she approached.

'You'll never guess what Mostafa has found!'

'Who's Mostafa?'

'He's my friend who works on the Nile cruise boat. The one who Mrs de Vere was rude to.'

'I remember now.'

'The boat got back late last night and found something floating in the wharf. Can you guess what it was?'

Lottie felt a flip of excitement. 'The case?'

'Yes!'

'Did they open it?'

'Yes.'

'And?'

'It was just full of papers.'

'What sort of papers?'

'Letters I think.'

'So Lord Harbottle threw a suitcase of letters into the river?'

'Yes.'

'I suppose we can't be sure it's the same case. We need to see it.'

'So let's go now!'

'Is it far?'

'It's at Bulaq, close to where he thew the case into the water. The tram can take us there in ten minutes.'

'I should tell Mrs Moore where I'm going.'

'Is she awake?'

'No, she's a late riser. In fact, if we're quick, I can probably get back here before she wakes.'

'Let's go then!'

THE MORNING AIR was pleasantly warm as they arrived at the riverside. Sail boats and cruise vessels were moored at the water's edge. Lottie followed Karim to a large passenger boat where he spoke with a wizen-faced man who didn't look a day under eighty but was hauling heavy ropes about. He pointed Karim to a scruffy stone building which the young man then disappeared into for some time.

Lottie strode up and down the water's edge and Rosie sniffed at the base of a straggly palm tree. She wondered what was keeping Karim for so long. Perhaps he'd discovered they were mistaken about the case and it wasn't the one which Lord Harbottle had thrown into the river after all. Her stomach gave a grumble, she was hungry for her breakfast. To add to her woes, the sun was getting stronger by the minute and she'd forgotten her sun hat.

Eventually, Karim emerged with the case in his hand, he gave Lottie a smile.

'Are you sure it's the same one?' she asked. 'It looks a darker colour.'

'It's been in the water, hasn't it? Come and have a look.' He carried the case to the shade of a tree and opened it. The contents were disappointing: a damp mound of paper coloured with streaks of blue and grey from where the ink had run.

Lottie bent down and examined the paper a little more closely. Some sheets were still dry enough to be pulled apart if done gently. One of them ripped a little as she pulled, so she continued as carefully as possible.

'You're going to try to read them?' asked Karim.

'I'm just looking for something which connects this case to Lord Harbottle.' Ink had smeared and smudged, but some words were decipherable. 'This definitely looks like correspondence,' said Lottie. 'Wait! I'm sure this letter is addressed to Margaret de Vere!' It wasn't easy to read, but the name was unmistakable. She looked up at Karim. 'It has to be the case he threw into the river! But what was he doing with Mrs de Vere's letters?'

As she pulled away the damp sheets of paper, she found drier letters in the centre of the heap. Fortunately, the case hadn't been in the water long enough for everything to be completely soaked through. There was a letter from a friend in England, which was relatively unscathed. Another letter from a friend was readable and also quite dull.

Lottie stood up for a bit, stretching out her cramped knees from where she'd been bent over the case. 'We're going to have to tell the police about this, aren't we? I don't know what it means, but I don't think Lord Harbottle can get away with throwing Mrs de Vere's personal letters into the River Nile.'

'Is there anything among them which looks interesting?'

'Nothing at all. Not among the ones I've managed to read, anyway.'

Karim cautiously peeled some more letters apart. 'I can speak English well,' he said. 'But I can't read much of it. The words on this letter are quite clear.'

Lottie stooped down again to have a look. 'It looks like a

note rather than a letter,' she says. 'There's no date or address on it.'

It was written in spidery black ink:

Dear Mrs de Vere,

I can only assume your recent letter to me was written in jest, for I struggle to believe a lady of your position would threaten to reveal information about a gentleman. Information which, in this case, is completely untrue. Furthermore, requesting money for your silence is simply vulgar and not the conduct I ever imagined you would be capable of.

I had thought better of you, and I'm extremely disappointed to discover I was wrong.

Please desist from contacting me any further on this matter.

Harbottle.

Lottie read the letter to Karim.

'What does it mean?' he asked.

'I'm not completely sure. But I think she was trying to blackmail him.'

Chapter Twenty-One

'MARGARET DE VERE was blackmailing Lord Harbottle?' said Mrs Moore. She sat at her dressing table, applying rouge to her cheeks. 'Are you sure about that?'

'The letter he'd written to her suggested she was.'

'But what was she blackmailing him about?'

'I don't know.'

'Where's the letter now?'

'In the case which has been given to the police.'

'Golly. It doesn't look good for Lord Harbottle, does it? So you actually saw him throw the case into the river?'

'Yes.'

'I can't believe you didn't tell me this yesterday.'

'I didn't really find the opportunity and, besides, you were busy celebrating your dinner invitation from Prince Manfred.'

'Oh yes.' She smiled. 'Only two days to go now!' She got up from her seat. 'We should get to breakfast before they stop serving. It's going to be rather awkward if we bump into Lord Harbottle though, isn't it? What do you say to a man you suspect of murder? I don't enjoy having to grapple with such things first thing in the morning. The only dilemma one should face at breakfast is which preserve to spread on one's toast.'

AFTER BREAKFAST, Lottie took Rosie for a walk in the sunshine, then met Mrs Moore on the terrace for morning coffee. They heard a motorcycle splutter to a stop out on the street, then Benjamin Villiers and Hugo Whitaker climbed the hotel steps and joined them.

Mr Villiers placed his unread books on the table. Lottie eyed *Egyptian Temples,* thinking it looked quite interesting.

'Have you heard the latest, Mrs Moore?' he said.

'Have they caught the poisoner?'

'If only!' He laughed. 'No, they've found a suitcase in the river containing Mrs de Vere's correspondence.'

'Really?' Lottie thought her employer did a good job of feigning surprise. 'What on earth was it doing there?'

'No one knows. But there's a suspicion the suitcase was used to carry off the jewellery from Mrs de Vere's room and the thief then discarded the case into the river because they had no use for it anymore.'

'That makes sense, I suppose.'

'Well, it's the best possible explanation, isn't it? Oh look, there are the Harbottles. I'll ask them to join us.'

'I'd rather you didn't,' said Mr Whitaker.

'Why not?'

'Because Harbottle and I almost came to blows yesterday!'

'Tempers often flare in this heat. The pair of you need to settle the disagreement with a gentlemanly handshake.'

Mr Whitaker pulled a grimace.

'What else can you do? Glare at each other for the rest of his stay in Cairo? Just stop paying so much attention to Polly Harbottle and all will be well. You can find yourself another lady elsewhere, there are plenty in Miss Omar's club.'

'That's where Harbottle finds other ladies, too.'

'Does he?' said Mrs Moore, her eyebrows raised.

'Whitaker was only joking,' said Mr Villiers. 'Weren't you Whitaker? Now let's get the Harbottles over here and sort it out. I can't bear disagreements.' He put two fingers in his mouth and gave a loud whistle. Lord and Lady Harbottle startled, then walked over.

'Good heavens, Villiers,' said Lord Harbottle. 'What was that whistle for? I'm a peer of the realm, not an errant hound.'

'Sorry Harbottle, I wanted to get your attention. I thought you and Whitaker here could shake hands after yesterday's disagreement. Whitaker's willing, aren't you, Whitaker?'

He nodded, got to his feet, and held out his hand.

'Very well.' Lord Harbottle's moustache gave a twitch, and he shook Whitaker's hand. 'A new page, eh? A clean sheet. Water under the bridge and all that.'

Lady Harbottle's expression remained frosty, but Lottie noticed she and Mr Whitaker continued to exchange glances.

More coffee arrived, and the mood lightened for a while. Jokes were made about Mrs Moore's future as the Princess of Bavaria and she took them all in good humour.

'Heard about the case they've pulled out of the river?' Mr Villiers said to the Harbottles.

Lord Harbottle's coffee cup paused between its saucer and his mouth. 'Case?' His voice squeaked a little. 'What case?'

Mr Villiers explained further and also mentioned his theory about it having been used to take the jewellery from Mrs de Vere's room. His explanation was long enough for Lord Harbottle to recover himself.

'I suppose that all makes sense,' he said when Mr Villiers had finished. He lounged in his chair as if he hadn't a care in the world. 'Where's the case now?'

'With the police. I suppose they could dust it for fingerprints to find out who handled it.'

'*Fingerprints*? Wouldn't they have been washed off in the river?'

'Now that's a good point, Harbottle. I suppose they must have been. Oh look, here comes Mr Mahmoud, the investigator chap now.'

Lord Harbottle gripped the arms of his chair. 'Really?'

But the stern-faced, silver-haired official didn't look at him, instead he approached Lottie. 'May I have a word, Miss Sprigg?'

She didn't like the fact everyone's face turned to her in surprise.

'Yes, of course.'

THE HOTEL MANAGER'S office had photographs of pyramids and temples on the wall. Mr Mahmoud sat behind the large desk and Lottie faced him on a little chair.

'So you're the young lady who saw the man throwing the case into the river?'

'Yes. How do you know that?'

'The boat crew told me. They said you went down to the river this morning and looked inside the case. You were with Karim, the boy who sells necklaces beneath the tree.'

'Yes.'

'So when did you see the man throw the case into the river?'

'Yesterday evening.'

'And where were you?'

'Near the Egyptian Museum. We walked past the tram stop to the river.'

'Did the man get off the tram?'

'I think so.'

'And what time was this?'

'About five o'clock.'

'And did you recognise the man?'

'I think so.'

'Who did you think it was?'

'I think it was Lord Harbottle.' Lottie sighed. The last time she'd given a name to an investigator, she'd been threatened. 'You won't tell him I told you his name, will you?'

'Very well.' But she wasn't sure if she could trust him.

'What did you see when you looked inside the case this morning?' he asked.

'A lot of damp paper. Some of it was dry enough to read.'

'What did you read?'

'Some letters from Mrs de Vere's friends and then there was a letter... actually, it was a short note. That was from Lord Harbottle.'

'What did the letter say?'

'I can't remember the exact words, but he was telling Mrs de Vere not to reveal information about him. He told her it was vulgar to ask him for money.'

'What do you think he meant by that?'

'I could be wrong, but I think she was trying to blackmail him.'

Mr Mahmoud gave a sombre nod. 'You've been very helpful, thank you Miss Sprigg. It would have been better if you'd told me you'd seen him throw the case into the river shortly after it happened. Keeping these things to yourself doesn't make my job any easier, you know.'

'I'm sorry, I wasn't sure if I'd been mistaken in thinking it was Lord Harbottle I'd seen throwing the case into the river.'

'Next time, you must let me know immediately.'

'Yes.'

'Now please don't discuss what you saw in that letter with anyone else. You leave it to me now, yes?'

'Yes, Mr Mahmoud.'

Lottie left the office feeling as though she'd been told off.

. . .

IN THE LOUNGE, Mayar Omar noticed Lord Harbottle stride past. She called out to him. When he turned in response, she wasn't surprised to see the scowl on his face.

'You've heard about the case?' she asked.

'Yes.' He kept his voice low.

'You should have put a brick in it to weigh it down.'

'The wonderful benefit of hindsight, thank you for that, Miss Omar. But no one can connect me to it, if that's what you're hoping. The fingerprints will have washed off in the river and the contents will be a soggy mush.'

'So I'm the only one who knows?'

'Yes. And don't forget what I know about you, too. You're compelled to keep quiet. In fact, now is a good time for me to ask again for those photographs. If you don't give them to me, there's something I can tell people about you.'

'Are you threatening me again, Lord Harbottle?'

'You've got yourself into your mess, Miss Omar, it's nothing to do with me.'

Chapter Twenty-Two

THE REST of the day passed uneventfully. Lottie kept expecting Lord Harbottle to be arrested, but he wasn't. Lord Harbottle seemed to expect it too because he was tense and talkative during afternoon tea on the terrace. Lady Harbottle looked glum and said little.

The mood remained uneasy at dinner and it wasn't helped by the addition of Miss Omar, who joked merrily with Mr Villiers, but seemed to have little to say to Lord Harbottle. Mrs Moore didn't seem to have fully forgiven Miss Omar for her performance with Prince Manfred and kept her interactions with her perfunctory.

Mr Whitaker seemed uncomfortable too and kept fidgeting with his bow tie and cufflinks. Lottie passed pieces of chicken to Rosie under the table and wished the next hour away.

'Fancy the Turf Club tonight, Harbottle?' asked Mr Villiers.

'No thank you, I'm rather tired. I think I shall retire early.'

'Probably a good idea, old chap. Think I might do the same myself. What about you, Whitaker?'

'A quiet evening for me, too. Without a doubt.'

'I'm going to sit in the lounge with a drink,' announced Lady Harbottle. She glanced at Hugo Whitaker, and he acknowledged her with a small nod.

'No one wants to visit my club this evening?' asked Miss Omar. 'I'm trying to encourage some ladies to attend. Mrs Moore?'

'No, thank you.'

'Never mind. Hopefully we'll have plenty of other guests this evening. I shall go and get myself ready.'

ALONE IN HIS ROOM, Lord Harbottle stood on his balcony and listened to the hum of conversation drifting up from the terrace below. The curtain was pulled across the door behind him and he hoped it would keep the evening's mosquitos out of the room.

They'd found the case. How had someone seen it in that enormous great river? It was the Nile! A vast river. He should have thrown it further in where the current was stronger, then it would have been carried away far quicker. And how had he not thought of putting a brick in it? He could only hope the letters were impossible to read. But they couldn't be! How else had the police known it was Mrs de Vere's case? Some of the letters must have still been legible. Hopefully not the ones he'd written to her.

He groaned and rested his hands on the balustrade. Burning the letters would have been a better idea, but how could he have done so in secret? The whole thing had been rushed and poorly thought out. But he'd only had a short window of time to fetch the letters from the old lady's room. Why had she even kept them? She'd probably kept everything, it was the sort of thing manipulative blackmailers did. Every little piece of information on someone could be used against them for financial gain. Hearing that her husband had gambled away the de Vere fortune explained her behaviour. She'd had no money other than the sums people paid her to stop her gossiping. What an awful woman she'd been.

The letters she'd sent him had been ripped into tiny pieces and flushed down the lavatory. He'd been too fearful of Polly finding them. Although maybe that mattered less now she had eyes for Whitaker. How he detested that man! What sort of chap ingratiated himself with another man's wife? And so obviously too! If he had a revolver, he'd challenge the man to a duel. And he'd win it too, just as his grandfather had done. He couldn't think of anything more satisfying than shooting Hugo Whitaker stone dead.

He held out some hope that his letters had been ruined in the river. The police may have found Mrs de Vere's name, but perhaps they wouldn't find his.

He breathed in a chestful of balmy evening air. Everything would seem better in the morning after a good night's sleep.

He pulled open the curtain and stepped into the room.

There was someone there.

'Hello,' he said. 'I didn't even hear you come in.'

Chapter Twenty-Three

'Surely it can't be true?' said Mrs Moore. 'Lord Harbottle dead?'

It had just gone eleven o'clock in the evening and most of the hotel guests were gathered in the lounge. Lottie cuddled Rosie on her lap and tried to make sense of what had happened. Word had spread that Lady Harbottle had found her husband on the floor of their room with a knife in his chest. She was currently speaking to the police about it.

'Another senseless loss of life,' continued Mrs Moore. 'Whoever did it must have known Lord Harbottle was alone in his room.'

'He announced to us at dinner that he was going to retire early,' said Lottie. 'And you, me, Lady Harbottle, Mr Villiers, Mr Whitaker and Miss Omar were present at the time.'

'Well, it's clear that neither you nor I murdered Lord Harbottle, Lottie, could it really have been one of the other four?'

'I suppose it must have been.'

Mrs Moore lowered her voice. 'I hope I'm not speaking out of turn when I say this, but Lady Harbottle is an obvious suspect, isn't she? She's the one who found him and I don't think all was well in the marriage, was it? There was that embarrassing to-do yesterday between Lord Harbottle and Hugo Whitaker, and didn't Mr Villiers mention something about Lord Harbottle and the ladies in Miss Omar's club? By the sound of things, the pair of them had been philandering and now we end up with this! More murder!'

Benjamin Villiers and Hugo Whitaker approached.

'Dreadful news.' Mr Villiers shook his head. 'Never in a month of Sundays would I ever have imagined something like this. Poor old Harbottle. What did he ever do to anybody?'

'And poor Lady Harbottle,' said Mr Whitaker. 'What a dreadful shock for her.'

'I'm still trying to understand what happened exactly,' said Mr Villiers. 'Old Harbottle went up to his room at what time? About ten o'clock?'

'Yes, I think it was about then,' said Mrs Moore.

'Then half an hour later, there's a dreadful din because poor Lady Harbottle has discovered old Harbottle with a knife in his chest. She was in the lounge until then, wasn't she?'

'Yes, she was,' said Mr Whitaker.

'Were you with her?'

'Only for a short while. You told me to stop paying her attention, didn't you?'

'Yes, I did. Oh, here she comes, now.'

Lady Harbottle was weeping, her shoulders were slumped and her arms folded. 'Why would someone do that to him?' she whimpered. 'My poor dear husband! I stepped into the room and there he was on the floor. How could someone be so barbaric?'

'It's completely dreadful,' said Mrs Moore. 'I'm sure the culprit will be caught. They can't get away with it!'

Miss Omar joined them. 'I was just about to leave for the

club when I heard what happened. How are you, Lady Harbottle?'

'In despair!'

'I'm not surprised. What a terrible thing to happen to such a good man.'

'Could the murderer be the same person who poisoned Mrs de Vere?' said Mrs Moore.

'I wouldn't have thought so,' said Miss Omar. 'One was murdered by poisoning and the other killed with a knife. It's unusual for a murderer to use two different methods.'

'Is it?'

'I would say we're dealing with two culprits, a woman and a man,' said Mr Villiers. 'The woman poisoned Mrs de Vere because women prefer poisoning as a method of murder.'

'Do they?' asked Mrs Moore.

'Yes, it's an established fact. A man, however, is more likely to choose a more brutal form of attack.'

Lady Harbottle let out a sob.

'I'm sorry, Lady Harbottle. I didn't mean to emphasise the word brutal there, but I think you understand my meaning. This has to be the work of a man. I think if a woman had stood there with a knife in front of old Harbottle, he would have quickly disarmed her.'

'Not necessarily,' said Mrs Moore. 'There could have been a scuffle with a knife and she managed to get the upper hand.'

'Oh please stop talking like this!' wailed Lady Harbottle.

'Yes, please do,' said Mr Whitaker. 'It's not nice for Polly to hear. The speculation must be left to the investigators. We don't have the facts of the case, nor are we experienced enough to speculate on why someone would do such a thing. But they have done, and it's extremely sad indeed.' He turned to Lady Harbottle. 'Your husband and I had our differences, but he was a wonderful man.'

'Oh thank you, Hugo.'

'You have every reason to have been extremely proud of him.'

'That's kind of you.'

'And I'm certain this whole sorry mess will be sorted out extremely quickly.'

'You're too kind Hugo.' She rested a hand on his arm.

Chapter Twenty-Four

'How did you sleep, Lady Harbottle?' asked Mr Mahmoud the following morning.

'Dreadfully!' She slumped in her chair, incredulous that he wished to interview her again. 'I've got nothing else to tell you. Can't you see how distraught I am? I've told you everything!'

'I realise this is upsetting for you, Lady Harbottle.' He was putting on a soft voice for her benefit. 'But I just need to check the details with you again.'

'And what about the murderer?'

'We will catch him.' He smiled. 'Or her. Now, when did you last see your husband?'

'When he retired for the evening.'

'And what time was that?'

'I don't recall looking at a clock at all, but I think it was about ten o'clock.'

'How sure are you of that?'

'Not very sure at all! As I told you, I wasn't looking at a clock when he said he was going up to our room.'

'Did your husband usually retire at that time?'

'No, it was quite unusual for him. He liked to stay up late

127

as a rule. Quite often he would go out, to the Turf Club and to some other clubs too, I suspect.'

'You suspect, or you know?'

'I know he liked to visit clubs where there were dancing girls. Miss Omar's club, for example. He wasn't completely honest with me about it because he feared I might disapprove.'

'There were secrets between you?'

'No secrets at all! I think my husband knew I knew he went to Miss Omar's club, if that makes sense. He went to similar places when we were at home in London.'

'And you disapproved?'

'Yes, I did, which was why he wasn't always honest with me about it. I don't think married gentlemen should go to clubs like that, but they can't help themselves, can they?'

She didn't like the way he was looking at her. She'd admitted there had been conflict in the marriage and now he seemed suspicious.

'Did you or your husband argue recently?'

'No.'

'Did you argue at all?'

'No.'

'We have evidence that your husband threw Mrs de Vere's case into the river.'

'What sort of evidence?'

'Someone saw him do it.'

'Who?'

'Miss Lottie Sprigg.'

'Really? What was she doing there?'

'She just happened to be in the area at the time. We also know it was your husband because he was trying to destroy some letters which he had written to Mrs de Vere.'

'He wrote her letters? Why?'

'Mrs de Vere was trying to blackmail him.'

'Blackmail?' Why hadn't Bartholomew told her this? 'Did he give her any money?'

'We don't think so.'

'Good. But what was she blackmailing him about?'

'We don't know yet. We suspect it might have been... well, you have admitted yourself, Lady Harbottle, that you knew your husband visited Miss Omar's club. And Miss Omar has told us he had an interest in...' She grew impatient with him as he searched for a tactful phrase. 'Some of the ladies there.'

She sighed. 'So Miss Omar knew what he got up to?'

'Yes, it seems so.'

'And she must have told Mrs de Vere! Then the old lady must have decided she could make some money from my husband! The pair of them are absolutely despicable! I hope they feel awful about what they've done!'

'Well, one of them is deceased.'

'I hope the other one feels awful then!'

'The fact that Mrs de Vere is deceased and was blackmailing your husband raises an interesting question.'

'What?'

'Did your husband poison her?'

'No! How dare you! He's just died and you're accusing him of murder!'

'I realise it's not a nice thought, Lady Harbottle, but we have to consider everything. Do you know if your husband took Mrs de Vere's jewellery as well as her letters?'

'No! He wouldn't have taken her jewellery.'

'We believe the jewellery and the letters were taken out of her room in that case. Perhaps he gave the jewellery to someone else before he threw the case into the river?'

'My husband was not a thief! I realise he took the letters, but that was because he was trying to protect himself. He clearly didn't want anyone finding out that awful woman was trying to blackmail him. Thank goodness he didn't give in to it.'

Lady Harbottle sat back in her chair and tried to slow her breathing. Had Bartholomew stolen the jewellery? What would he have done with it if he had? She had thought she'd known her husband well, but now she was discovering things he'd kept from her. Perhaps she hadn't known him at all?

'Can you remind me of the time you went to your room last night?'

'Yes, it was half past ten.'

'Who were you with until that time?'

'Mrs Moore and Miss Sprigg.' She had to hope the pair of them couldn't recall the exact time she'd left them.

'And when you got back to your room—'

'There he was! It was dreadful!' She gave out a wail and sank her head into her hands, hoping this would end the interview.

Chapter Twenty-Five

'I CAN FEEL another headache coming on,' said Mrs Moore. They sat on the terrace with Mr Whitaker, Mr Villiers and Miss Omar.

'Don't give in to it!' said Mr Villiers. 'Drink some more coffee, that will sort it out.'

'I think coffee makes it worse.'

'No, it definitely makes it better.'

Lady Harbottle drifted towards them, her pale face made ghostlike by the contrast with her black dress.

'Polly,' said Mr Whitaker, his voice filled with concern. He pulled out a chair and helped her sit in it.

'I shall tell you all everything,' she said. 'Because I don't want any gossip or speculation about poor Bartholomew. He threw Mrs de Vere's case into the river because it contained letters written by him asking her to stop blackmailing him.'

This was met with gasps.

'She was blackmailing him?' asked Mr Villiers.

'Yes. He didn't tell me about it and I'm upset that I didn't know, I suppose he had his reasons for keeping it from me.

When she died, he used the opportunity to remove all evidence of her blackmail.'

'But why did he want to remove it?' asked Mr Whitaker.

'It would have made him an obvious suspect! People would have thought he'd murdered Mrs de Vere to keep her quiet. I know he wouldn't have done such a thing. My husband wasn't perfect, but he wasn't a murderer. But it was quite a shock to learn that he'd taken the case of letters and I didn't realise that Miss Sprigg saw him throw it into the river.'

Everyone turned to Lottie and she felt her face burn. 'That's right,' she said.

'Were you following him?' asked Lady Harbottle.

'No! Why would I do that? I just happened to be walking by the river and I saw him.'

'What an odd coincidence,' said Mr Villiers. He turned to Lady Harbottle. 'How did he get hold of the case and the letters?'

'He must have gone to Mrs de Vere's room as soon as she was taken ill and removed them. I wondered why he disappeared for a short while that morning. People were trying to help her and he said he had to go to the room to fetch something. I didn't even ask him what it was, I was too distracted by what had happened to Mrs de Vere.'

'So he stole the jewellery too?' said Mr Whitaker.

'I don't believe my husband took those jewels.'

'He must have done. Presumably he went into the room, found an empty case to put all those letters into and noticed the jewellery while he was doing so. He must have put that in the case as well.'

'He wouldn't just steal valuable items for the sake of it.'

'Maybe he gave them to someone as a gift?' said Mr Whitaker.

'Who?'

'I don't know. Maybe he owed someone something and decided to give them the jewellery instead.'

'My husband would never have been in debt to anyone.'

'Perhaps his murderer thought he stole the jewellery?' said Mr Villiers. 'Maybe he was murdered in revenge for taking it?'

'No, I don't think so,' said Lady Harbottle.

Lottie thought it odd that she was so convinced of what she did and didn't believe.

'I'm sorry, Polly, but I think your husband must have taken that jewellery,' said Mr Whitaker. 'There can't have been two people dashing to Mrs de Vere's room the moment she fell unwell.'

'Bartholomew was not a thief! He only went to that room to rescue his good name.' She turned to Miss Omar. 'You colluded with Mrs de Vere to blackmail my husband!'

'I'm sorry? I did no such thing!'

'How else did Mrs de Vere know he had been visiting your club?'

'I don't know, but it wasn't me who told her. Mrs de Vere and I fell out with each other a couple of months ago. I had no interest in sharing any information with her after that. Why would I? What would I gain from it?'

'Money?'

'I had no need for money like she did. She tried her hardest to ruin me, but it didn't work.'

Lady Harbottle angrily turned on Mr Villiers. 'Then it was you!'

'Me, Lady Harbottle?'

'Yes, you knew where my husband was going each evening because you took him in your motorcycle's sidecar.'

He shifted in his chair. 'This is a little bit awkward. I can't deny, Lady Harbottle, that your dear departed husband and I frequented Miss Omar's club on a couple of occasions. I must admit that I once let slip to Mrs de Vere...'

'So that's how she found out!'

'It must have been, I'm sorry. But I certainly didn't get involved in any blackmail of any sort. That's really not my style at all.'

'Visiting a club seems a fairly innocuous thing to bribe a man about,' said Mrs Moore. 'Surely there was more to it than that?'

'I think there was...' Mr Villiers trailed off and gave Lady Harbottle a wary glance.

'Another woman?' she said with a sigh. 'I knew what he was like.'

'So how did Mrs de Vere find out about that?' asked Mrs Moore.

'Once again, I...' Mr Villiers rubbed his brow. 'It was a slip of the tongue.'

Lady Harbottle sighed again. 'What's done is done. And none of this gets to the bottom of who murdered my husband and who murdered Mrs de Vere. It's all so terribly confusing. Did Bartholomew's death have something to do with the blackmail or not? And what else did he keep from me? Can anyone here tell me that? I feel an awful lot of secrets are being kept. I hope none of you here now are withholding information from me! If you are, then I sincerely hope it comes back to haunt you. I need you all to be completely honest with me now. And we need to do absolutely everything we can to find out what happened to my husband!'

Lottie couldn't decide whether this was a genuine plea or a speech by a murderer to cover their tracks.

Chapter Twenty-Six

'WHAT DO you want from me now, Hassan?' said Mayar Omar. 'You don't think I had anything to do with Lord Harbottle's death, do you?'

'I've told you before that you must call me Mr Mahmoud when we're doing these interviews.'

'But that sounds so formal! And quite silly too when you consider how long we've known each other.' She smiled at him sweetly, but he was clearly in no mood for her charm.

'What were you doing between ten o'clock and half past ten yesterday evening?'

'So you *do* think I had something to do with it!'

'I'm asking everybody the same questions, Miss Omar.'

'That must be terribly boring for you, Hassan. Aren't you fed up with asking everyone the same thing while sitting here in the manager's little office?'

'Yes, I am, as a matter of fact. I'm fed up with not being able to catch the person who has murdered two people in this hotel. Now, are you going to help me, Miss Omar? Or are you going to waste my time? I must warn you that if you're going to waste my time, then there will be consequences.'

'I don't like seeing you this grumpy, Hassan. I think you've been working too hard over the past few days.'

'Just tell me where you were between ten o'clock and half past ten yesterday evening.'

His mood would probably improve once she answered some of his questions, so she decided to be as helpful as she could. 'I was in my room, getting ready for my evening at the club.'

'You live in this hotel now?'

'Not all the time, I told you before, Hassan, that I have noisy neighbours.'

'What time did you go to your room?'

'About a quarter to ten.'

'And what time did you leave?'

'About half past ten, I was just stepping out of the door when I heard the staff responding to reports of screaming.'

'Screaming?'

'It was Lady Harbottle, she'd just arrived back at her room and found her husband dead.'

'So you were in your room for forty-five minutes?'

'Yes.'

'Alone?'

She gave a smile. 'Why do you ask?'

'Because I want to know if anyone else can vouch for the fact you were there the entire time.'

'I was! Don't you believe me?'

'I don't know when you're telling me the truth, Mayar.'

He was using her first name now. He'd dropped the formality, but she didn't like the serious tone of his voice. 'What do you mean by that?'

Mr Mahmoud reached down behind the desk and lifted a small wooden box. He placed it on the desk in front of her. 'Have a look inside.'

She didn't like the arrival of the box. Was he going to catch her out?

Reluctantly, she leaned forward and lifted the lid. Light twinkled on the diamond necklaces, rings and bracelets inside the box.

'Do you recognise these items, Mayar?'

She gave a nod and felt her shoulders slump. There was no use in pretending anymore.

'Can you tell me what they are?'

'Jewellery.'

'I know you can be more specific than that.'

'Mrs de Vere's jewellery.'

Chapter Twenty-Seven

'MISS OMAR IS THE MURDERER?' said Mrs Moore as they gathered for afternoon tea on the terrace.

'She's the person who stole Mrs de Vere's jewellery,' said Lady Harbottle. 'So she must be.'

'How do they know she stole the jewellery?'

'I heard they found a young man trying to sell the items in the Khan el-Khalili bazaar,' said Mr Whitaker. 'He admitted to the police that Miss Omar told him to sell them for her.'

'Why would she do that?' said Mrs Moore. 'She wasn't short of money, was she?'

'Perhaps she was,' said Mr Villiers. 'There's no doubt her club had been quieter recently, but when I mentioned it to her, she denied it.'

'Karim told me his brother's friend works as a waiter at the club,' said Lottie. 'Apparently Miss Omar has been worrying about money and how to pay her staff.'

'I'm impressed with how you discover information like that, Lottie,' said Lady Harbottle. 'You happened to be present when my husband threw the case into the river and you also learned that Miss Omar's club was struggling.' She gave Lottie a stony look.

'So Miss Omar was short of money!' said Mrs Moore. 'Who'd have thought it? Fewer people were visiting her club because Mrs de Vere had been saying unpleasant things about the place. She must have been driven by revenge and the opportunity to make some money from Mrs de Vere's jewellery.'

Lady Harbottle turned to Mr Villiers. 'You were with Mrs de Vere when she was poisoned, did you see Miss Omar put something in her cup?'

'I remember she came to the table and spoke to me, she also said a brief hello to Maggie. I didn't actually see her put anything in the cup, but I wasn't watching out for it. She clearly did it with a good sleight of hand so that neither I nor Maggie noticed. She's a clever lady.'

'Not so clever if she's been caught out,' said Mrs Moore.

'She would have got away with it if the man they caught in the market hadn't told them,' said Lady Harbottle.

'So Miss Omar murdered Mrs de Vere,' said Mr Whitaker. 'Why did she also murder Lord Harbottle?'

'I really don't know,' said Lady Harbottle, shaking her head. 'Perhaps he knew something.'

Mr Villiers cleared his throat. 'I'm aware of a slight disagreement between them.'

'Really?' said Mrs Moore.

'Yes. This isn't easy for me to say as it's a rather delicate matter...' He grimaced and looked at Lady Harbottle.

'Go ahead, Benjamin. Whatever it is, I'm ready to hear it.'

He inhaled deeply on his cigarette then began. 'Well, a few days ago, I took Harbottle down to Miss Omar's club because he wanted a word with her about some photographs.'

'What sort of photographs?'

'Harbottle was talking to a... I'll be frank here, I hope you don't mind Lady Harbottle. But he had a girl on his knee and a chap took some photographs of them. Harbottle was most concerned about who would see the photographs, for understandable reasons. He asked me to take him down to the club so he could ask for them. From what I understand, Miss Omar wasn't wonderfully responsive to the request. If you ask me, she was having photographs taken of clients in compromising positions just in case she needed to make use of them.'

'What a horrible woman!' said Lady Harbottle.

'And although I don't want to speak ill of someone so recently deceased, I'd say your husband's behaviour was pretty horrible too, Polly,' said Mr Whitaker.

'Thank you, Hugo.' She pursed her lips. 'It's not nice to hear, but it's important we know the truth.'

'Why would Miss Omar wish to make use of the photographs?' asked Mrs Moore. 'Not more blackmail?'

Mr Villiers shrugged. 'Perhaps that was her plan, we know she needed the money. It seems you can't trust anyone, can you?'

'I still don't understand why she murdered Lord Harbottle,' said Mrs Moore. 'He wanted the photographs, and she refused to give them to him. So why did she murder him?'

'Perhaps she didn't want him telling people she was taking photographs of her guests in compromising situations,' said Mr Whitaker.

'But if she didn't want him doing that, why not just return the photographs as he requested?' said Mrs Moore. 'I don't fully understand her motive.'

'There has to be something more to it,' said Lady Harbottle. 'And I can only hope I can speak to her and get a full explanation for why she's done what she has. The woman is despicable!'

Lottie glanced about, wondering where Rosie was. She looked around her chair, then under the table.

There was no sign of her.

She felt her heart thud as she looked around more earnestly.

'Is there something the matter, Lottie?' asked Mrs Moore.

'Have you seen Rosie?'

'She was with us just now, wasn't she?' She glanced around the terrace through her lorgnette.

'What is it?' said Lady Harbottle.

'We've lost sight of Rosie,' said Mrs Moore. 'She can't have gone far.'

'Oh dear,' said Mr Whitaker, glancing about. 'Does she do this often?'

'Not very often,' said Lottie. 'But sometimes she takes herself off if she's distracted by another dog or food.'

Everyone now began looking about them.

'Rosie!' Lottie called out. This prompted people at neighbouring tables to look too, and soon the waiters were also helping.

A sickening sensation weighed in Lottie's stomach. 'Where is she?'

'Don't panic, don't panic,' said Mr Villiers. 'She won't have strayed far.'

Lottie's head spun as she dashed about the terrace, desperately hoping to catch sight of the brown and white corgi. She went into the lobby and asked at the reception desk, but no one had seen her.

'Oh no!' She stood in the centre of the lobby, her palms on her cheeks, wondering where she should go or what she should do next. Was Rosie in the hotel? Or had she left? Had she decided to walk herself to Ezbekiya Garden?

A waiter approached her. 'The footman says he saw two men with a dog.'

'Two men? Where did they go?'

'He saw them leave the hotel.'

Lottie ran out to the steps and leapt down them, two at a time.

'Wait, miss!' A footman called to her.

'I need to get my dog!'

'We have men going after them,' he said.

'Where did they go?'

'That way,' he pointed to the left. 'But you must not follow, it's a dangerous neighbourhood. Our staff will get her back.'

Lottie stared down the street, willing them to return with Rosie.

'Someone took her? I don't understand!'

Were they planning to sell her? What if she never saw Rosie again? She couldn't bear the thought. 'I need to get her, she'll be frightened!' She made a move, but the footman gently held her arm. 'No, miss. It's not safe. Just wait here and hopefully news will come soon.'

Lottie felt her knees buckle, then she slumped to the ground. 'Oh Rosie! I hope they don't hurt her!'

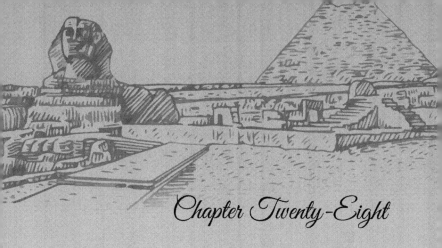

Chapter Twenty-Eight

'I HAVE TO DO SOMETHING,' said Lottie. She lay on her bed and Mrs Moore sat next to her, holding a damp cloth to her forehead.

'Leave it to the hotel staff, Lottie. They know their way around Cairo. The footman was quite right to stop you, you can't go running about the place on your own.'

'I can't just do nothing! I need to go out and find her. Why haven't they got her yet?'

'I'm sure they're doing all they can, Lottie.'

'Why would someone take her?'

'I suppose they liked the look of her and wanted her as a pet of their own.'

'They can't just take someone else's dog!'

'I know, but there are some strange people about, Lottie. Now try to get some rest.'

'It's impossible!'

'I know, but if you don't, then you'll tire yourself out completely. I'm sure they'll find Rosie, they saw the men who took her, didn't they?'

The footman had reported the thieves as being two

Egyptian men. One short and slender and the other tall and wide. Lottie could only hope these vague descriptions would lead to someone recognising them.

A knock at the door made Lottie leap up.

'Rest,' said Mrs Moore, putting a hand on her shoulder. 'I'll go to the door.'

Lottie's heart pounded as she watched her employer answer the door to a maid. Had Rosie been found? As each second ticked by, Lottie realised she hadn't been.

'A letter addressed to you, Lottie,' said Mrs Moore, closing the door and handing her an envelope.

Lottie tore the envelope open. Inside was a brief note:

Your dog will be returned to you if you agree to leave Cairo. Please arrive at Cairo railway station tomorrow and board the midday train to Alexandria. You must be in possession of a ticket to travel and you must be on board the train and the dog will be returned. Do not tell the police.

The note was unsigned.

'What does it say?' Mrs Moore asked.

Lottie handed her the note, still trying to comprehend it.

'Someone's kidnapped Rosie?' said Mrs Moore. 'What a disgrace! I'm going to find out who's behind this!' She marched out of the room.

Lottie remained where she was. Someone had taken Rosie because they wanted her to leave. She must have upset somebody. The murderer?

Miss Omar was the murderer. She must have instructed the two men to take Rosie. But how had Lottie angered her? She'd told Mr Mahmoud she'd seen Lord Harbottle throw the case into the river and she'd had a few discussions with Karim about who'd been acting suspiciously. How else had she caused trouble?

Lottie consoled herself that she had some idea about what had happened to Rosie. She hadn't been stolen, and she wasn't going to be sold. She was going to be returned to Lottie if she left Cairo. But would the kidnapper keep to their word?

Mrs Moore returned after a little while. 'It's no use, I can't find out who left this note. The man at the reception desk says a scruffy messenger boy ran in and left it on the counter. He ran off before anyone could challenge him. Someone wants you to leave Cairo, Lottie. Have you been snooping about again?'

'Not as much as I did in Paris. I've been careful.'

'Well, someone fears you and they want you to leave.'

'It could be Miss Omar, couldn't it? If only we could ask her what she's done with Rosie.'

'I don't see how we can, she's been arrested. The police might allow us to speak to her but then we'd have to explain to them our reason for doing so and the note says we shouldn't contact police. I think for Rosie's sake, we should obey the note. We don't want her coming to any harm.'

'But what if they don't return Rosie to me? All we have is their word.' Despair consumed Lottie as she imagined leaving Cairo on a train without her beloved dog. 'I'll do anything to get her back. Anything!'

'I know, and so would I. The person who's written this note says Rosie will be returned to us tomorrow at midday.'

'I suppose I shall have to book a ticket and turn up at the train station at that time. I shall have to leave.'

'We'll both have to leave, Lottie.'

'But you can't! You're having dinner with Prince Manfred tomorrow evening!'

'I'm sure he will understand if I don't go.'

'But you've been waiting for weeks to have dinner with Prince Manfred! That's the whole reason we're here in Cairo! I can book a hotel in Alexandria and stay there until you're ready to join me.'

'I won't let you travel alone, Lottie, I insist on coming with you.'

'But what about Prince Manfred?'

Mrs Moore squeezed her hand. 'Prince Manfred can wait.'

There was another knock at the door. Mrs Moore answered.

'Lottie...' she said, seeming unsure. 'The street hawker boy is here.'

Lottie wiped her eyes with her handkerchief and smoothed her hair as best she could. 'You mean Karim?'

'Yes. What do you want, Karim?'

'I'd like to speak to Lottie about Rosie.'

'Alright, come on in.'

Karim fidgeted with his hands as he stood at the end of Lottie's bed. 'My brother Ahmed helped chase after the men,' he said. 'But he lost them in the Birka.'

'Where's that?' asked Lottie.

'It's on the other side of the Ezbekiya Garden, there are lots of little streets there. I'm going to go and have a look for them.'

'You must be careful!' said Lottie. 'They might be dangerous!'

'I'll be careful. I'll get some other friends to help too. We need to make sure we can get your dog back.'

'I don't want you to take any risks. I've received a note from the kidnappers saying they will give Rosie back to me if I leave Cairo. I have to be at the train station at midday tomorrow.'

'Leave Cairo? I'm sure there's no need for you to do that. We can find your dog.'

'Thank you Karim, but promise me you'll be careful?'

'Of course. I'll let you know how we get on.'

'What a helpful young man,' said Mrs Moore after Karim had departed. 'We can only hope he has some success with it.'

. . .

LOTTIE DIDN'T FEEL like eating that evening. She stayed in her room. Sleep would be impossible. She arranged the mosquito net around her bed and tears rolled down her face as she looked at the spot where Rosie had slept each night.

Where was she now? She was probably lonely and scared. Would the kidnappers give her any food? Would she have something to drink? An image of Rosie cowering in the corner of a filthy room made Lottie sob again. She wanted nothing more than to go out onto the streets and find the dog for herself.

Chapter Twenty-Nine

AFTER A SLEEPLESS NIGHT, Lottie got up early, dressed and went down to the hotel reception to find out if there was any news on Rosie. If there wasn't, then she and Mrs Moore would need to pack their belongings and prepare to leave Cairo.

Lottie felt responsible for ruining Mrs Moore's dinner with Prince Manfred. If she hadn't angered the murderer, they wouldn't have kidnapped her dog. If only she'd kept out of it! It was all her fault.

The man at the reception desk was sympathetic, but said he'd received no news of Rosie being found. Despondent, Lottie walked out onto the terrace where the early morning sunshine warmed her face.

She descended the steps to the street which was quiet at this hour. A man leading a donkey acknowledged her with a nod, but there was no one else around. She looked to the right, hoping to see Karim standing beneath his tree, but it was presumably too early for him to be up and about.

She thought about Rosie, hoping her dog had managed to

eat and sleep. Was she frightened? It was difficult to imagine her not being.

'Lottie!'

She spun round at the sound of her name and saw Karim coming from the opposite direction she'd expected.

'I was just coming to find you!' He was out of breath, but she was encouraged by the smile on his face. 'We think we know where Rosie is and who's got her.'

'You do!' Lottie's heart skipped.

'Ahmed and I knocked on every door we could and we found someone who'd heard a dog barking from a house they'd not heard barking from before. We've found out who lives there and we think his name is Ali. My brother says he's a cousin of his friend Tarek.'

'Is he certain about that?'

'I think so. And if it is Ali, then we have little to worry about. He's harmless.'

'Even though he took my dog?'

'Someone must have paid him to do it.'

'The doorman told me there were two men.'

'We think it could be his friend Sayed.'

'The doorman said one was short and slender and the other tall and wide.'

'Apparently Ali is tall, so that fits.'

'And you say he's harmless?'

'Yes, both of them are. They're just idiots who would do this sort of thing for money.'

'I hope they don't hurt Rosie!'

'I'm sure they won't. And I think it will be quite easy to get Rosie back from them,' said Karim.

'How?'

'We can come up with a plan to distract them.'

'Distract them? How?'

'I'll explain it all in a moment. Do you think you can help us?'

'Yes! Just tell me what I need to do.'

'You will need to be in disguise because you might receive too much attention as a tourist.'

'What sort of disguise?'

'Just some clothes which will help you fit in, my sister has some you can borrow.'

KARIM'S SISTER lived in a small, neat house in a narrow street where laundry hung between the buildings and a group of barefoot children played with a dog. His sister spoke a little English but mainly communicated through smiles as she helped Lottie put on a blue linen robe over her blouse and skirt. A long blue wrap then went over her head and shoulders and Karim's sister helped her with a blue silk veil which covered her nose and mouth. With only her eyes visible, Lottie felt well-disguised.

'Good luck!' said Karim's sister as they left. They were joined by Ahmed who was older and broader than his brother and a little less handsome in Lottie's opinion.

'I have to be at the hotel for half past seven to prepare breakfast,' he said. 'Hopefully, this will be quick.'

'Thank you for helping me,' said Lottie.

'I just do what Karim tells me to,' he said. 'Even though he's younger and smaller than me, I'm still scared of him.' They laughed.

Lottie felt butterflies in her stomach as they made their way through the maze of streets. She had put her trust in Karim and his belief that the kidnappers, Ali and Sayed, were harmless. But was he right?

She was nervous about what could happen, but she was also excited by the prospect of seeing Rosie again.

Traders were setting up their stalls selling fruit and bread. A variety of smells, both good and bad, assaulted Lottie's nostrils. After a walk of ten minutes, they stopped in a dusty street where most of the windows and doors were shuttered.

Lottie's stomach twisted in knots. Karim and Ahmed had told her their plan and now she could only pray it would work.

'This is the house,' said Ahmed, pointing to a shabby wooden door.

'Are you ready?' Karim gave her a smile.

'As ready as I'll ever be.'

'Here goes.'

Ahmed launched into a tirade of shouting at his brother, Lottie couldn't understand a word of it. Karim then responded, and their loud voices echoed around the street. Lottie stepped away as shutters began to open, the brothers were intimidating even though she knew it was just an act.

An old lady shouted at them from a balcony up above. Then a door opened further down the street, and a stocky man stepped out and stared at them.

The wooden door of the house didn't open. But Lottie startled as she heard a dog bark from behind a shuttered window. Rosie! Her bark was immediately recognisable. How could Lottie get her out of there?

She wanted to call out to Rosie, but she had to remain silent for now. The plan was to entice the occupants out of the house, and Lottie was beginning to worry it wouldn't work. She noticed Karim glancing at the house as if realising no one had yet come to the door. Meanwhile, an angry-looking man was striding down the street towards them, shouting. This was concerning. The pretend argument could soon become serious.

Karim then stooped to the ground, picked up a stone and hurled it at the wooden door. Lottie's mouth felt dry with fear, she was sure this would cause trouble. Moments later, the door was flung open and a tall young man stepped out. Lottie guessed this was Ali. The angry man had reached them and now four men were shouting at each other.

Lottie edged closer to the open doorway. Where was Sayed? Was he in the house? Could she really bring herself to go in there knowing he could be inside?

Rosie barked, and the shouting continued. Karim and his brother now shoved each other a little bit. More people were emerging from their homes and a lady with a broom handle was striding purposefully towards them. The pretend disagreement would have to end soon before someone got hurt.

Now was Lottie's chance.

She took in a deep breath and moved up to the doorway. She peered inside, but it was too dingy to see much. She had to be brave and step inside.

The door opened directly into a single room with rough walls. She saw a table with two chairs and an iron bedstead covered with a faded blanket.

Rosie was tied to the bedstead with a rope. Her tail wagged cautiously, as if she was unsure what to make of the robed and veiled visitor.

Lottie dashed over to her. 'It's me, Rosie!'

The corgi gave an excitable bark and her tail wagged so hard that her whole body wiggled.

Lottie bent down and tried to untie her dog as quickly as she could. Her fingers grew sore as they struggled with the knot in the rope. The argument outside appeared to be dying down as a lady's voice sounded over the men's. The lady with the broom handle was presumably sorting everyone out. Lottie sensed she had little time left.

She pulled at the piece of rope and Rosie tried to lick her face through the veil.

'I've nearly got you, Rosie.'

Finally, the rope was free, and Lottie gathered Rosie up

into her arms. She got to her feet, turned to the door, and found her way blocked by a slender young man. Presumably this was Sayed. He stared at her, wide-eyed.

Lottie held her breath and stared back. What should she do now?

Sayed wasn't advancing towards her, nor was he threatening her. She did the only thing she could think of. 'Get out of my way, Sayed!' she shouted as loudly as possible. Rosie joined in with a bark.

To Lottie's surprise, he stepped aside and stared at her, open-mouthed, as she dashed out of the door.

She kept expecting someone to stop her, but no one did. She ran as fast as she could through the maze of streets.

Chapter Thirty

'GOOD GOLLY!' exclaimed Mrs Moore as Lottie arrived at her room with Rosie in her arms. 'Why are you dressed as an Arab lady and where on earth did you find Rosie?'

Lottie told her what had happened.

'You did all that before I even had my breakfast? You could have been seriously hurt! How dangerous, Lottie. You should never have attempted such a thing!'

'Karim told me there was nothing to be scared of, I was nervous but he was right in the end. So this means we don't have to leave Cairo today and that you can have dinner with Prince Manfred this evening.'

Mrs Moore smiled. 'Yes I suppose so. And I'd already made a start on my packing! I hope you didn't risk everything saving Rosie just so I could dine with Prince Manfred. We could have rearranged it.'

'I rescued Rosie because I was worried about her and I feared the kidnappers wouldn't keep their end of the bargain when we went to the train station.'

'And how is she?'

'She seems fine. She doesn't seem frightened at all.'

'Well I'm relieved it worked out alright, Lottie, but it could have gone horribly wrong and you could have been harmed or even murdered! Imagine that! Please promise me you won't attempt such a thing again? Although it worked out well this time, you might not be so lucky next time.'

'I hope there won't be a next time.'

She placed Rosie on the floor and the dog went over to greet Mrs Moore. Lottie slumped into the chair by the window.

'I did something foolish though.'

'What?'

'I completely forgot to ask the kidnappers who'd told them to take Rosie.'

'You didn't have the chance to ask them, did you? From the sound of things, you had to get Rosie then leave as quickly as possible. And besides, it must have been Miss Omar who paid them, mustn't it?'

'I suppose it must have been.'

'You must tell the police what happened this morning and then they can arrest those young men too. Despicable people!'

Chapter Thirty-One

To Lottie's surprise, Mayar Omar was sitting with Lady Harbottle, Benjamin Villiers and Hugo Whitaker at breakfast.

'The police have released her?' Mrs Moore whispered to Lottie as they approached the table.

'I can tell by your expression, Mrs Moore, that you're surprised to see me here,' said Miss Omar. 'I've just begun explaining to everyone that I'm a thief, but not a murderer.'

'Is that so?'

Lottie and Mrs Moore took their seats.

'You found your dog, I see,' said Lady Harbottle. 'Where was she?'

'She'd strayed away from the hotel and a street trader found her,' said Lottie.

'Well, that's a bit of luck,' said Mr Whitaker. 'You must be very relieved.'

Lottie kept Rosie on her lap as she listened to Miss Omar.

'I stole the jewellery from Mrs de Vere's room,' she said. 'I'm not proud of myself. I saw an opportunity to make some much-needed money for my club. And who better to steal from than the lady who had been depriving me of an income?'

'I thought you said she had no effect on your business?' said Mr Villiers.

'It was a lie, I'm afraid. I had to pretend all was going well, otherwise people would have suspected I was bitter towards her and had a motive to murder her. I wanted to believe she hadn't affected my business at all, but I'm afraid she had.

'As soon as I saw she had fallen unwell at breakfast, I saw my opportunity to get hold of her jewellery. It was good news for me when people suspected Lord Harbottle had taken the jewellery. It was kind of him not to tell the police that he saw me doing it.'

'He saw you?' asked Lady Harbottle.

'Yes, we both arrived at Mrs de Vere's room at the same time. I'd been planning the theft for a while and had managed to take a spare key to her room from the manager's office. Lord Harbottle, however, was prepared to break the door down as he was desperate to get hold of his letters to her. He couldn't believe his luck when he found me there with the key, I told him I would admit him to the room only if he promised not to breathe a word to anyone. He kept his word, and I kept mine. Once it was revealed Mrs de Vere had been poisoned, we hoped that our actions would be blamed on the murderer.

'It was unfortunate that the case was pulled out of the river, he should have weighed it down with a brick! And when he was accused of taking the jewellery, I wondered if I should speak up. But I needed the jewellery so I could sell it to help my business. But I also made a mistake, I chose a young man to sell the jewellery who gave my name away. I was angry about it, but my actions were foolish in the first place. I brought it on myself.'

'But you had a good motive for murdering both Mrs de Vere and Lord Harbottle,' said Mrs Moore. 'You could have poisoned Mrs de Vere because you wanted to silence her and steal her jewellery. You could have murdered Lord Harbottle because he saw you take the jewellery.'

'Yes, I realise I could be a suspect. All I can ask is that you take me at my word. Fortunately, it's what Hassan Mahmoud, the investigator, has done. I'm lucky that we're old friends.'

'So that's why the police let you go!' said Mr Villiers.

Her eyes darkened. 'He let me go because I'm innocent of murder! I've admitted to the theft and I'll be punished for it. But you must believe me when I tell you I'm innocent, I could never harm another person in that way. I admit I've lied and deceived people, but I would never commit murder. Why would I risk losing everything I've worked so hard for? I came to Egypt to seek my fortune, and it was going well until I fell out with Mrs de Vere. But I told myself that once I had a little money, everything could recover again.'

Lottie believed Miss Omar. She wasn't a murderer.

But that meant the murderer was still at large. Surely he or she was going to be angry that Lottie had rescued Rosie and wouldn't be leaving Cairo?

She gave a shiver and cuddled her dog even closer. She didn't feel safe.

AFTER BREAKFAST, Lottie helped Mrs Moore choose the outfit to wear for dinner with Prince Manfred that evening.

'What about this one?' Her employer held up a pink and white gown with a large red collar and an enormous bow. 'Actually, I think it's a little too daytime. There's this one.' She pulled out of the wardrobe a grass green silk dress with enormous sleeves. 'Actually, the neck is cut a little too low, I don't want the prince to think I'm being too forward.' She put it back. 'I must make sure I read some of *Colloquial German* today, with everything that's been going on over the past few days, I've neglected it. Apparently, Prince Manfred is trying to learn English.'

'For your benefit?'

Mrs Moore gave a giggle. 'Well, that would be wonderful, wouldn't it? But I don't think he's doing it just for me, I suspect he's realised that a knowledge of English is extremely useful.' She turned back to her wardrobe. 'Now, I do like this one.' She held up a sky blue dress trimmed with purple ribbons. 'Perhaps it's a bit fussy? And dare I say it, old-fashioned. Oh, this is so difficult! And what if I end up wearing the same colour as Prince Manfred? It would be most embarrassing, Lottie. He enjoys wearing lots of colour, doesn't he? If only there was some way of knowing what he was going to wear.' She bit her lip, and Lottie sensed a request was forthcoming. 'Would you mind calling at his suite, Lottie, and enquiring what colour the prince plans to wear this evening? It's so important that we're coordinated.'

Lottie smiled. After the dramatic events of the morning, this task seemed simple.

'Alright then.'

A GERMAN-SPEAKING gentleman answered the door of Prince Manfred's suite, and neither he nor Lottie could understand each other. 'Boris,' he said, pointing to the floor.

'Boris?' Lottie looked down at the carpet, wondering what he was pointing at.

'Boris.'

It took Lottie a moment to realise he was referring to someone who was downstairs. She wondered if he meant the blue-suited interpreter.

She gave him a smile. 'I'll speak to Boris. Thank you.'

. . .

LOTTIE SEARCHED the reception area and lounge before going out onto the terrace where Lady Harbottle and Mr Whitaker were enjoying a cup of coffee together. Mr Villiers was presumably nearby because his books were on the table.

'What have you done with Mrs Moore?' asked Mr Whitaker.

'She's deciding what to wear for her dinner with Prince Manfred this evening. I've been tasked with finding out what colour he's wearing, so she doesn't clash with him.'

Mr Whitaker laughed, and even Lady Harbottle raised a smile. Lottie glanced about and saw the blue-suited interpreter talking to one of the waiters. Was he Boris? She lingered for a moment and waited for the conversation to end.

Mr Villiers' book, *Egyptian Temples*, caught her eye again. She picked it up and flicked through the pages, hoping to find some interesting pictures in it.

'This is a library book,' she said, noticing a stamp on the flyleaf which said, "Property of Guildford Library". She turned the page and noticed the book had been borrowed three months previously. 'Mr Villiers must be running up a large library fine,' she said. 'He can't return this any time soon.'

Mr Whitaker chuckled. 'That's going to be an enormous fine by the time he returns it!'

Boris the interpreter was still talking to the waiter, so Lottie turned more of the pages. As she did so, a slip of card fell out onto the floor. She bent to pick it up and saw that it was a library card for Guildford Library. It had a name on it, but it wasn't Benjamin Villiers.

'Another tour arranged!' said Mr Villiers as he approached them, rubbing his hands together in satisfaction. 'Oh, hello Miss Sprigg! What are you doing with my book?'

She'd already replaced the library card in the book and hoped he hadn't noticed her looking at it.

'I'm interested in Egyptian temples,' she said, handing the book back to him.

'Are you indeed? Well, any time you'd like to know more about them, just ask.'

'Thank you, Mr Villiers.'

Boris the interpreter had finished talking to the waiter, he strolled past and she managed to speak to him.

'What colour is the prince wearing this evening?' he replied. 'He can't decide. What colour is Mrs Moore wearing?'

Chapter Thirty-Two

'SO HAVE you finally decided which colour you're wearing tonight, Mrs Moore?' asked Mr Whitaker at lunch.

'Yes, after some toing and froing with his interpreter, Boris, we've decided on pink for me and green for him.'

'Lovely,' said Mr Villiers. 'You'll make a delightful couple.'

'Thank you, Benjamin. I wouldn't describe us as a couple though, we're merely having dinner together.'

'You will be the envy of all the ladies in Europe.'

'I don't know about that!'

'Ah, but you will. He's Europe's most eligible bachelor, is he not?'

'So say some.' Mrs Moore turned bashful.

'I'd like to find out how the evening goes,' said Lady Harbottle. 'Hopefully I shall see you before I depart for England tomorrow?'

'You're going home tomorrow? I shall make sure I see you before you leave.'

'I'm going back to England too,' said Mr Whitaker.

'Really?' said Mr Villiers. 'I thought you wanted to come with me on my next tour to the Valley of the Kings?'

'Another time, Villiers. It has been suggested that my companionship may be helpful at this difficult time.' Mr Whitaker turned his gaze to Lady Harbottle and a grin spread across Mr Villiers' suntanned face.

'Ah, I see!' he said. 'You didn't waste any time, did you, Whitaker?'

'I beg your pardon?' Mr Whitaker wasn't smiling. 'What exactly do you mean by that?'

Mr Villiers stopped smiling too. 'It was just a joke, Whitaker. Apologies if I caused offence.'

Mr Mahmoud the investigator arrived at their table and greeted them. 'May I request an interview with each of you this afternoon?' he asked. 'I have obtained some more information about the recent crimes and I need to speak to you all individually.'

'Again?' protested Lady Harbottle.

'What can we possibly tell you that we haven't already?' asked Mr Villiers.

'An utter waste of our time!' said Mr Whitaker.

Lottie felt her stomach turn. Before lunch, she had tucked two pieces of paper into her skirt pocket and she was wondering when the right moment would come to tell people about them.

'I realise this isn't convenient for any of you,' said Mr Mahmoud. 'However, I must insist on it, especially as some of you have plans to return to England tomorrow. It is of the utmost importance that we do our best to establish exactly what happened to Mrs de Vere and Lord Harbottle.'

'Perhaps I can help,' said Lottie.

Everyone looked at her. She glanced down at Rosie, wary of their gaze. The dog looked up at her and she gave her a stroke.

'You would like to speak with me in the office?' said Mr Mahmoud.

'No, it's alright. Everyone can hear what I have to say.'

'Very well,' said Mr Mahmoud. 'What is it?'

'I know who the murderer is,' she said, her heart thudding. 'It's Mr Villiers.'

'WHAT?' exclaimed Benjamin Villiers. 'Have you lost your mind, Miss Sprigg? Who are you anyway? Just a little maid girl who runs about doing things for an heiress. Have you any idea who you're talking to here? You need a lesson on how to respect your superiors, you—'

'Enough, Villiers!' said Mr Whitaker. 'Stop being obnoxious and let's hear the girl's reasoning.'

'I'm interested to hear it,' said Lady Harbottle.

'Do go on, Miss Sprigg,' said Mr Mahmoud.

Lottie cleared her throat. 'Well, the most obvious clue is that Mr Villiers was sitting with Mrs de Vere at breakfast when the poison was put into her tea. Even though other people visited the table that morning, he had the best opportunity to administer it.'

Mr Villiers laughed. 'And that's your reasoning, Miss Sprigg? Have you any idea how regularly I was questioned by *him* on that point?' He pointed at Mr Mahmoud. 'He thought exactly the same! I can't tell you how much explaining I've had to do over the past few days just because of the inconvenient fact I happened to be sitting at the same table as poor old Maggie when she was poisoned. I was simply in the wrong place at the wrong time.'

Mr Mahmoud spoke next. 'Miss Sprigg, the fact that Mr Villiers had the best opportunity to poison Mrs de Vere doesn't mean he did it.'

'I realise that.' Lottie caught Mrs Moore's eye. Her employer gave her an encouraging smile. The pair had already discussed the two pieces of paper and Lottie knew that Mrs Moore was supportive of her theory. But Lottie also knew it was going to be quite a task to convince everyone else she was right. 'I had a look through one of Mr Villiers' books earlier,' she said. 'It's called *Egyptian Temples*.'

'That's this book here for anyone who's vaguely interested,' said Mr Villiers, pointing at it.

'It's actually a library book,' said Lottie.

'A very overdue library book,' added Mr Whitaker.

'I can assure you all that failing to return a library book on time is the biggest crime I've ever committed,' said Mr Villiers. 'And I don't see how the book is relevant to anything.'

'Do go on, Miss Sprigg,' said Mr Mahmoud.

Lottie continued, 'While I was looking through the book, a library card fell out. I saw the name on the card was Victor Hawkins.'

'A stolen library book then?' said Mr Whitaker. 'Or a stolen library card?'

Mr Villiers lit a cigarette and gave a nonchalant smile.

'I recognise the name Hawkins,' said Lottie. 'It was Mrs de Vere's maiden name.'

'How do you know that?' asked Lady Harbottle.

'Madame Chapelle told me. She was a friend of Mrs de Vere's and told me a little bit about her family.'

Mr Whitaker turned to Mr Villiers. 'You were related to Mrs de Vere?'

'Do I look like I was related to her?'

'No, but you haven't answered my question.'

'I think Mr Villiers could be related to Mrs de Vere,' said Lottie.

'There are lots of people with the name Hawkins!' he retorted.

Lottie persevered. 'When I spoke to Madame Chapelle, she didn't know who would inherit Mrs de Vere's fortune. She was a widow and had no children or siblings. In those circumstances, the estate can pass to a distant relative.'

'Villiers here is a distant relative?' asked Mr Whitaker.

'He could be. He could even be Mrs de Vere's heir.'

'Then why murder her?'

'The only reason I can think of is that he wished to inherit her fortune sooner rather than later.'

Lady Harbottle gasped. 'Heavens above! Really?'

Mr Whitaker turned on Mr Villiers. 'So out with it then, are you a Hawkins?'

Mr Villiers exhaled a cloud of smoke. 'I will admit to you all now that my name is, in actual fact, Victor Hawkins, just as it says on my library card. A card I thought I'd lost but had, in fact, left in one of my books. Perhaps I should be grateful to you, Miss Sprigg, for locating it for me. It will come in useful when I return *Egyptian Temples* to the library.'

'So you have used a false name!' said Mr Mahmoud. 'And that's the reason you don't look like your passport photograph. It isn't your passport!'

'A stolen passport now?' said Mr Whitaker. 'So the book and the library card were not stolen but the passport is?'

Mr Mahmoud continued, 'It's not actually you in the passport picture, is it, Mr Hawkins? Who does the passport belong to?'

'Well it's quite obvious that it belongs to Benjamin Villiers. He lent it to me.'

'It is an offence to travel using someone else's passport.'

'Who's Benjamin Villiers?' asked Mr Whitaker.

'A friend.'

'So you lied to me, Villiers? Or I suppose I should call you Hawkins now.' He had a wounded expression. 'And to think I considered you a true friend!'

'I *am* a true friend!'

'Not if you lied to me about who you really are.'

'I can prove to you that I'm a true friend!'

Mr Whitaker shook his head sadly and Lady Harbottle rested a comforting hand on his shoulder.

'I may have shared a surname with Mrs de Vere,' said Mr Hawkins. 'But I had no reason to murder her. Or old Harbottle for that reason.'

'Miss Sprigg,' said Mr Mahmoud. 'I'm very impressed with what you have found out, but none of this proves that Mr Hawkins is a murderer.'

Lottie pulled the two pieces of paper out of her pocket. 'Perhaps these will help. When my dog was taken from me yesterday, I received a note telling me she wouldn't be returned to me unless I agreed to leave Cairo.'

'Oh my goodness!' said Lady Harbottle. 'Your dog was kidnapped?'

'Yes, and I have the note here,' said Lottie, unfolding it. 'I think the person who wrote it attempted to disguise their handwriting, but they didn't do a particularly good job. I can see a lot of similarities with this note here.' She unfolded the second piece of paper. 'This is a list of Cairo's sights which Mr Hawkins wrote for Mrs Moore.'

'Let me see,' said Mr Mahmoud, peering over her shoulder.

'The handwriting is slightly different,' said Lottie. 'But the ink is exactly the same.'

Mr Mahmoud gave a nod. 'I would say they were both written by the same person.'

Mr Hawkins gave a snort. 'You're accusing me of murder *and* kidnapping your dog, Miss Sprigg? What next?'

'Drop the act, Hawkins!' said Mr Whitaker. 'It's all looking rather damning if you ask me. Why not be a gentleman and tell us exactly what's been going on? There's no use in digging a hole for yourself, you'll merely end up deeper in it. We'll all think a lot better of you if you come clean.'

Mr Hawkins scratched his chin and said nothing.

'Hawkins!' said Mr Whitaker. 'Just a moment ago, you told me you could prove you are a true friend. How about you prove it now? Swallow your pride and tell me the truth like a proper gentleman. Perhaps I may retain a modicum of respect for you if you can give me a thorough explanation. But if you continue your lies, then I will consider you unfit to even lick the dirt off my boots!'

Mr Hawkins puffed up his chest, clearly keen to improve Mr Whitaker's opinion of him. 'Fine,' he said. 'I have an explanation.'

Mr Whitaker sat back in his chair, his arms folded. 'Excellent. Then let's hear it.'

Chapter Thirty-Four

'Mrs de Vere was my father's cousin,' said Mr Hawkins.

'You murdered a member of your own family?' asked Mrs Moore.

'Can I explain it properly without being judged at every step? I realise it looks bad, but please hear me out. Margaret's father and my father's father were brothers.'

'So Miss Sprigg was on to something!' said Lady Harbottle. 'Are you Mrs de Vere's heir?'

'Yes, Lady Harbottle. Now I know it seems heartless to poison one's own flesh and blood, but I barely knew her! And also my hand was forced.'

'How?'

'My father cut me out of his will and I had debts to pay.'

'Why did he cut you out?' asked Mrs Moore.

'Because he thought I was profligate. A load of baloney if you ask me. The trouble with the older generation is that they don't understand how expensive modern living can be. I worked in the family furniture business, but I ran up a few debts in some card games and my salary didn't cover them. I confessed this to my father and, instead of helping me out, he cut me out of his will! He called me irresponsible, feckless... and some other names I can't repeat in front of the ladies. But you get the picture. My father died last year and everything went to my sister! Can you think of anything worse? She has no need for it at all, she's married to a dull lawyer and between them they're worth a fortune.' He paused and dabbed his eyes. 'I was left out in the cold.'

If Mr Hawkins wanted people to feel sorry for him, Lottie suspected he was failing.

'And then I remembered something,' he continued. 'Many years ago, my father's cousin, Margaret de Vere, visited us. I was only a boy, about knee high to a grasshopper at the time. She and my father weren't close, and I don't believe I ever saw her again after that visit. At some point during my boyhood, I recalled being told I was the sole beneficiary of her will. I didn't give this much thought until I was disinherited and then I did a little research. How excited I was to discover that Margaret had married a rich man!'

'And that's when you decided to murder her?' asked Mrs Moore.

'No, now hold on. It's not quite that simple. I reiterate the fact I had met her so long ago that I had no fondness for her. I don't believe she had any for me either, she certainly didn't know who I was when we met here in Cairo. Had she been a doting family member who'd taken a great interest in me during my boyhood, then obviously I wouldn't have poisoned her.

'When I found out she was in Cairo, I decided I could find work in Egypt and that would help pay for my passage. I'd read a lot about Tutankhamun's tomb in the papers and I'd always fancied myself as the Howard Carter type. So I read a few books on the topic and decided to be an archaeologist.'

'So you actually know nothing about archaeology at all?' said Lady Harbottle.

'I read some books on it.'

'Anyone can do that!'

'I know.'

'So you're not a proper archaeologist.'

'Another lie, Hawkins?' said Mr Whitaker. 'Did you also lie about the digs you'd been on in Mesopotamia and Syria?'

'I'm afraid I did. But I'd read about it all in books and I remain very interested in going on a dig at some point in the future. I wasn't completely pretending.'

'But you're not an archaeologist,' said Lady Harbottle. 'Despite all your talk when you took me and Bartholomew to Luxor and the Valley of the Kings.'

'No, I'm not. But I discovered you don't need a great deal of knowledge to show people about. You can tell a group of tourists about an ancient site and most of them aren't listening to a word you're saying anyway. They're more interested in exploring it for themselves and taking a few photographs, and then they want to know when lunch is and when they can have a nice cold drink. I knew I could make a bit of money doing it and that's what I did while getting to know my father's cousin.'

'Disgraceful,' said Lady Harbottle.

'When did you change your name?' asked Mr Mahmoud.

'I did it while I was in Alexandria, before I got to Cairo. I realised I had to assume a new identity because there was a risk Maggie would recognise the family name and work out who I was. So I stole a passport of a man I met in a hotel bar in Alexandria. I plied him with drink, helped him back to his hotel room and stole his papers.'

'So Benjamin Villiers wasn't a friend?' asked Mr Whitaker.

'No. Just a drunk tourist. And can I just mention that, at this stage, I did consider not murdering Margaret. I had a thought that I could befriend her and then introduce myself as her long lost heir. But I soon discovered she wasn't the most amenable of ladies. In fact, I think she completely disliked me, despite my best efforts. There was a risk she could write me out of her will once she discovered who I was. So there was only one thing for it, I had to poison her with arsenic.'

'You *had* to?' said Mrs Moore.

'Yes, what else could I do?'

'Where did you find the arsenic?' asked Mr Whitaker.

'You can buy just about anything on the streets of Cairo if you know where to look.'

'But your entire plan was pointless, wasn't it, Hawkins?' said Mr Whitaker. 'Because it transpired that Margaret de Vere didn't have a fortune at all. Lord Harbottle heard from a former land agent that Francis de Vere ran up enormous gambling debts and his wife had to sell the estate after his death to pay them all off.'

Mr Hawkins wiped his brow. 'That was a severe blow. I think I hid my reaction to that dreadful piece of news quite well. To discover I had murdered Mrs de Vere in vain was extremely sobering indeed. I can only take comfort from the fact that she isn't particularly missed by anybody. Can anybody honestly say that they miss Mrs de Vere?'

'You can't just take someone's life!' said Mrs Moore.

'I regret doing it now because I'm in a great deal of trouble. But the lady was old and troublesome, and all I wanted was to inherit my fortune sooner to pay off my debts.'

'And what about my poor husband?' asked Lady Harbottle. 'Why did you murder him?'

Chapter Thirty-Five

'Your *poor husband*, Lady Harbottle?' said Mr Hawkins. 'The man you felt so much affection for that you were actually with Whitaker at the time of his death?'

'How dare you!'

'I think it's quite convenient for you and Whitaker that Lord Harbottle is no longer around.'

'I loved my husband! What a nasty man you are!'

'Polly's right,' said Mr Whitaker. 'So stop the taunting and tell us why you murdered him.'

'To save you, Whitaker! My true friend!'

'To *save me*?'

'I was in a troublesome situation. Look, I didn't want to harm old Harbottle. I was extremely fond of him as you know and we socialised together and had a lot of fun. But he gave me an ultimatum.'

'What?' asked Lady Harbottle

'The trouble was, he saw me dropping the arsenic into Mrs de Vere's cup of tea. I know it was a brazen act and I suppose I'd been a bit arrogant about my ability to do it in a public place and not be spotted. I really thought I'd got away with it. But he made things awkward for me.'

'By doing what?'

'He told me to do something for him and I couldn't do it.'

'What?' said Mr Whitaker.

'You don't want to hear.'

'I *do* want to hear.'

'Well, I don't think Lady Harbottle would believe me.'

'Just come out with it.'

'Very well, then. He told me I had to poison someone who was causing him a bit of bother.'

'Who?'

'You, of course, Whitaker.'

Mr Whitaker paled. 'Me?'

'My husband asked you to poison Mr Whitaker? Impossible!'

'Quite possible I'm afraid, Lady Harbottle. He didn't like the fact Whitaker had designs on you and he wanted him out of the picture. He told me if I didn't go ahead with the plan, then he would tell the police he'd seen me put poison into Mrs de Vere's tea. It turns out old Harbottle was more ruthless than I realised. I don't suppose you knew he had it in him, did you, Lady Harbottle?'

'I think you're lying.'

'If only I was! Having committed murder once, please believe me when I say I didn't want to do it a second time. But I realised I had to murder one of my friends. Either Whitaker or Harbottle. What an awful dilemma I was in! So I spent a day or two in absolute torment. And then I told Harbottle I would do the deed just so he would leave me alone. After that, I had to weigh things up in my mind. Having discovered I was going to receive no inheritance whatsoever, I knew I had to make money myself. Whitaker and I'd had some interesting conversations about going into business together and so my friendship with him was quite advantageous. As for Harbottle, if I carried out his wish, he would then know I'd murdered two people. Just think what he could have done with that information! He could have used it against me at any time. So I decided that if I murdered Harbottle, not only would no one know I was a killer, but I could also go into business with my friend Whitaker and hopefully sort out my money troubles.

'And so my decision was made. I crept into the hotel kitchen one night and stole a knife. I wasn't happy about it, let me tell you. But what else could I do? As luck would have it, Harbottle retired early the other evening and his wife was distracted by Whitaker. I saw my opportunity and seized it. He'd left his bedroom door unlocked, presumably because Lady Harbottle was due to join him. He was out on the balcony when I tip-toed in and... oh dear I am sorry.' He covered his face with his hands. 'Forgive me, Harbottle. It was either you or my friend Whitaker!'

'Horrific,' said Lady Harbottle. 'And so horribly cruel.'

Mr Hawkins recovered himself, then inhaled on his cigarette. 'I'm afraid that cold, hard logic determined my decision, Lady Harbottle. And I really am very sorry that your husband met his end in the way he did. If only I could have done things differently. If only someone could understand the dilemma I was in, I fear that Pharaoh's Curse got me after all.'

'No it didn't,' said Lady Harbottle. 'It was nothing to do with the curse at all, it was your own doing.'

'And you organised the kidnap of our beloved dog, Rosie!' said Mrs Moore.

'That's because I grew wary of Miss Sprigg! She seemed to know things about people and I didn't like it. I reasoned that it wouldn't be long before she worked things out so I needed her to leave Cairo. I paid that pair of ruffians to take the dog, but they didn't exactly do a good job of it, did they? They were about as effective as the chap Miss Omar paid to sell the jewellery in the bazaar. If you want a job done properly, you have to do it yourself. That's how the old saying goes.'

'What a cold-hearted, brutal man you are, Mr Hawkins,' said Mrs Moore. 'I don't think I've ever met anyone quite so selfish.'

He stubbed his cigarette out in the ashtray. 'I don't know what else to say. And I'm not going to argue with you, Mrs Moore. I think you've just given a very accurate description of my character.'

Chapter Thirty-Six

LOTTIE WAS READYING herself for bed that evening when a
knock sounded at her door. She answered and a grinning Mrs
Moore swept in, a vision in pink.

'Oh Lottie, what a wonderful evening I've just had!' Her
wide gown took up most of the room. 'The prince is such a
dear! I don't believe I've laughed so much in years!'

'I'm happy you had such a good time.'

'Oh, I did! I could have learned a little more German
beforehand, Boris had to do all the translation. The man's
voice must be hoarse by now!'

'What did you talk about?'

'Oh, anything and everything. Dreams, hopes, desires...
and the prince has many funny stories. The tricks he used to
play on his governesses! The family went through so many of
them, they lost count. Anyway, I realise the hour is late but I
want to speak to you now as we need to get packing in the
morning.'

'For where?'

'Monaco! That's where Prince Manfred is off to next. And
thankfully he's told me himself this time, I haven't had to find

it out from someone else. There's a sailing from Alexandria the day after tomorrow. So we must spend tomorrow night in Alexandria. Isn't it exciting?'

'Yes.' Although Lottie felt pleased for her employer, she'd been hoping they could stay a few days longer to see more of Cairo. 'Don't you want to see a few sights before we leave?'

Mrs Moore scowled. 'The ones on Mr Hawkins' list? I've got no interest in anything that murdering miscreant recommends. Anyway, I'd far rather see Monaco now. It's a principality, you know.'

'What's that?'

'I don't know. I think it means that it's a country but a tiny one. Anyway, I'm sure I won't sleep tonight because I'm too excited! Can I just say again how proud of you I am, Lottie?'

'Thank you, Mrs Moore.'

'Don't look so bashful, I mean it! Mr Villiers, or Hawkins, or whoever he is, nearly got away with two terrible crimes. And yet you managed to catch him out! All with a little bit of skill and ingenuity. I was singing your praises to the prince earlier.'

'I'm sure there was no need.'

'Oh but there was! He's very impressed with your skills and he thinks you're quite marvellous. Anyway, I'll leave you to get some sleep now, Lottie. I'll see you in the morning for another adventure!'

THE FOLLOWING MORNING, Lottie took Rosie out to the gnarled tree near the hotel. Karim stood in the shade with his stall of necklaces. He gave her a grin as she approached and Rosie pulled on the lead, eager to see him.

'Thank you for rescuing Rosie yesterday,' said Lottie. 'You don't know how grateful I am.'

Karim patted the dog on the head. 'It was no problem, the plan worked out well in the end, didn't it? Once you'd left with her, Ahmed and I immediately explained to everyone why we'd done it. Most people found it funny in the end.'

'And Ali and Sayed?'

'The police arrested them and I hear the murderer's been caught now.'

'That's right, Benjamin Villiers, the archaeologist. That's what we knew him as, but he's really Victor Hawkins. His father was Mrs de Vere's cousin.'

Karim shook his head. 'I quite liked him, that goes to show how good I'd be at finding a murderer.'

'You were very helpful. And sadly, I've come to say goodbye.'

His face fell. 'You're leaving?'

'For Monaco.'

'That's a shame. But I hope you have a nice time.'

'I'm sure I will. I want to stay in Cairo a bit longer, but my employer wants to leave today.'

'I'd like you to stay in Cairo a bit longer, too. I enjoyed our day together.'

'Me too.' They exchanged a smile, then Lottie opened her purse. 'I'd like to thank you by buying a necklace. You stand out here all day every day and I've not bought a single thing from you.'

'You don't have to.'

'But it's how I want to repay you.'

'You don't need to repay me with anything! Friends help each other, there's no need to pay or repay people. Which necklace do you like the best?'

A white and blue beaded necklace with a little silver scarab had caught Lottie's eye. 'That one,' she said. 'How much is it?'

Karim unhooked it from the display. 'It's free.'

'No it's not!'

'For you it is.' He held out the necklace. 'Lean forward and I'll put it over your head.'

Lottie did so. 'I want to pay you for it,' she said as he placed the necklace around her neck.

'And I'm refusing your money,' he replied with a smile.

'So there's nothing I can do to say thank you?'

'Just saying it is enough. But perhaps there's one thing you can do.'

'Yes, what is it?'

'Whenever you wear this necklace, perhaps you can remember who gave it to you?'

Lottie felt tears prick the back of her eyes. 'Of course, Karim! I'll never forget you! And neither will Rosie.'

'Thank you.' He gave the dog another pat. 'I wish you both well on your travels. And if you ever come back to Cairo, come and find me under this tree.'

'I will Karim. I promise.'

THE END

Thank you

Thank you for reading *Murder in Cairo*. I really hope you enjoyed it! Here are a few ways to stay in touch:

- Join my mailing list and receive a FREE short story *Murder in Milan*: marthabond.com/murder-in-milan
- Like my brand new Facebook page: facebook.com/marthabondauthor

A free Lottie Sprigg mystery

Find out what happens when Lottie, Rosie and Mrs Moore catch the train to Paris in this free mystery *Murder in Milan*!

Lottie and Mrs Moore are travelling from Venice to Paris when their journey is halted at Milan. A passenger has been poisoned and no one can resume their trip until the killer is caught. Trapped in a dismal hotel with her corgi sidekick, Lottie is handed a mysterious suitcase which could land her in trouble...

Events escalate with a second poisoning. Lottie must clear her name and find the killer before the trip is cancelled for good!

Visit my website to claim your free copy:
marthabond.com/murder-in-milan

Or scan the code on the following page:

Murder in Monaco

Book 4 in the Lottie Sprigg Mystery Series.

Life's a gamble on the risky Riviera!

Lottie Sprigg and her employer arrive in glitzy Monaco where Lottie finds a mysterious note which threatens murder. Before she can act on it, a body is found in a private room at the Monte Carlo Casino.

Who wrote the note? Lottie takes a gamble on discovering their identity. But as she and her dog Rosie navigate a web of lies, new dangers emerge.

Lottie has her work cut out in a place where money means power. Monaco may be fashionable and glamorous, but the hairpin bends on its twisty roads can be very perilous indeed...

Find out more: mybook.to/monacomurder

Printed in Great Britain
by Amazon

21523323R00114